SNOWED IN WITH MR. HEARTBREAKER

A BRO CODE NOVELLA

PIPPA GRANT

Editing by Jessica Snyder, HEA Author Services
Proofreading by Emily Laughridge & Jodi Duggan
Cover Design by Qamber Designs
Cover Image Copyright © Wander Aguiar

Cash Rivers, aka a movie star who cannot get this ray of sunshine out of his head

THE LAST TIME I was at a holiday party this awful, a loose pet tiger, a malfunctioning smart home system, and undercooked chicken were involved.

On a private island.

With auto-locking doors that left me trapped with the pet tiger and an upset stomach in a room rapidly chilling to below freezing.

Not exactly where a kid who grew up in a middle-class family in a city near the Blue Ridge mountains in southern Virginia ever would've expected to find himself, but life's interesting sometimes. One day, you're a normal kid goofing off and making a music video with your buddies to post on YouTube for fun. The next, you're in a world-famous boy band. Then those boy band days are over, you move to Hollywood, and you're getting invited to places only the richest of the rich and most famous of the famous hang out.

This party, however, is awful for a different reason.

And possibly far more interesting.

In the bad way.

"I'll bite," Davis Remington, my childhood friend and former boy band buddy from our Bro Code days, says over a bottle of holiday kombucha. We're lingering in one corner of the living room of our friend Beck's weekend mountain mansion, which looks like it was decorated by an overzealous tipsy elf.

"What's with the grumpy face?" he asks.

"I'm not *grumpy*. I'm *thoughtful*."

He slides a look at me and smirks.

With his brown man bun, thick beard, and tattoos, he's more often mistaken for an underfed, lost lumberjack than he is for anything else.

"Thoughtfully staring at your pool house tenant," he says.

Asshole's not wrong.

I'm very much staring at my pool house tenant.

I would've thought being all the way across the country from my house in Malibu and its accompanying pool house that Aspen Bowen has rented out for the past year would mean I wouldn't have to see her.

Think about her.

Hear her.

Watch her.

Feel like a creepy old dude who needs to get his shit together and quit obsessing over a woman who's fifteen years younger than I am.

"She's blocking the dart board," I tell Davis.

He keeps staring at me.

Doesn't have to say a word.

I know what he's thinking.

Whole damn game room with another dart board in the basement.

"So ask her to move," he says.

There are roughly a dozen people between Aspen and me. All of them are my family, or they're friends close enough to be considered family. People I don't see often enough. I should be chatting with more of them instead of hiding in the corner with Davis.

But I'm not merely hiding in a corner with Davis. I'm hiding in the corner so I can watch Aspen. She's a rising pop star, invited to our annual hometown get-together by virtue of being tight with Waverly Sweet, girlfriend of Fireballs' second baseman and future baseball hall-of-famer Cooper Rock, who's always invited because he lives next door to Beck and all of us are rabid, lifelong Fireballs fans.

"Don't want it that bad," I lie.

I want *her*.

I want her bad.

"Uh-huh," he says as Aspen's laughter carries across the living room, over Elvis's "Blue Christmas," accompanied by the scents of cinnamon and ginger from the cookies the kids and grandmas are baking in the kitchen.

The multicolored lights strung around the window illuminate Aspen's soft brown hair, and my cock twitches every time she takes a drink off of her mug of spiced cider then follows it with a lick of her lips.

3

"You remember the time you wouldn't let anyone else touch the blue darts and you convinced Tripp you'd swallowed them so the rest of us couldn't have them?" I say to Davis.

He almost grins. Almost, but not quite. "Wasn't as hard as it should've been."

"We should take a road trip together. Get another tour bus. Pack up all five of us. See the country. Recreate the fun, but do it where we can stop and see shit."

He takes a swig off his beer. "No."

"We can get a bus with two bathrooms instead of just one. I know you like your own bathroom."

He slides me another look. "Or you deal with your real problem and quit trying to pick fights to avoid thinking about it."

"Life's great. No problems here."

He looks Aspen's way as she squeals "Commander Crumpet!" loudly enough for half the house to hear.

I don't have to look to know who Commander Crumpet is.

I helped her find Commander Crumpet a new home when she texted me around the first of the year, asking if I'd be around while she was gone on her first big road trip. She needed a babysitter for her pet hedgehog. Little beastie didn't do well on car rides, she said, but he was very well-behaved when he was at home.

Timing didn't work, but it was obvious she was going to have a bigger problem than needing a temporary babysitter for her carsick-prone hedgehog soon.

She didn't realize it—or maybe she was in denial—but I saw the writing on the wall.

Between Aspen's inherent talent and then her endorsement from Waverly, she was on track to being home less and less often because she'd be more and more in demand around the country.

But now Commander Crumpet lives with my buddy Levi, his wife, and their kids. Considering their first family pet was a squirrel, Commander Crumpet has been much easier on all of them.

And he's spoiled as hell.

"Aww, how's my sweet baby?" Aspen croons at the little creature. "You look so happy."

Shit.

I know that catch in her voice.

I shouldn't. I shouldn't have spent nearly enough time with her to know that catch in her voice. Especially since our schedules mean we're rarely in California at the same time, much less in the same city.

But it doesn't take long to catch an obsession.

"You wanna go downstairs and—" I start, turning to Davis, but he's not there anymore.

Shit.

I've been staring at Aspen so long that I didn't even notice Davis left me to look like a solo creeper in the corner.

Fuck this.

I might be too old for her, but that doesn't mean I can't be polite. I drop my empty beer bottle in Beck's recycling bin, then head across the room, making small talk with my siblings and friends and their older kids on the way.

And eventually, I reach Aspen.

She's chatting animatedly with Zoe, Levi's oldest stepdaughter and primary caregiver for Commander Crumpet. I nod to the hedgehog in Zoe's hands.

"Has he been good enough for Santa to bring him presents this year?"

Zoe rolls her eyes as only a preteen can. "He's a hedgehog, Uncle Cash."

Aspen looks up at me. She's maybe five-six. Brown hair tied up in a ponytail that I'd like to—ahem. Dressed in all black. Hazel eyes dancing.

"He gets presents all year round, don't you, Commander Crumpet?"

The hedgehog doesn't answer, but he does sniff at her.

"Such a good boy," she says.

"He's the best," Zoe agrees.

"Does he still like to sleep in socks?" I ask.

"How do you know how he likes to sleep?" Zoe asks as Aspen glances at me again.

Fuck me, she's pretty.

And fifteen years younger than you, you dirty old man.

I tilt my head toward her as I answer Zoe. "Aspen told me."

"You forgot Hudson's name the last time you were in town, but you remember how a hedgehog likes to sleep?"

Not my best moment, and I have a feeling she won't ever let me forget that I forgot her little brother's name. "I was jetlagged, and I'd spent the past three months working on *Hollow and Hunter*. With Judson Clarke."

"So what did you call Hudson?" Aspen asked me.

I clear my throat. "Juntson."

She grins, and it makes the twinkling holiday lights

seem brighter, the baking cookie scent more delicious, and the entire holiday season more magical.

"That must've been some epic jetlag."

"Shot the whole film in Australia."

"Oh, I've never been to Australia! Is it pretty?"

"Yeah. Very pretty. The whole country. I'll take you next time I go."

I realize what I've just said—and implied—and freeze in my tracks like I'm seventeen with my first crush instead of nearly forty with an inappropriate crush.

Zoe looks at me.

Then at Aspen.

Then pointedly back at me. *Do not be an old creeper with my second-favorite pop star, Uncle Cash, or I will tell my stepdad to destroy you.*

Was I this observant when I was in middle school?

She's still in middle school, isn't she?

"She's busy," Zoe deadpans.

"Hey, Zo, Waverly's looking for you," Levi calls across the room.

And there goes Zoe.

Not even a goodbye.

Just a high-shrieked squeak accompanied by, "Waverly's finally here?" and she's gone, taking the hedgehog with her.

"Hope you didn't want to see Waverly too," I joke to Aspen.

"We hung out earlier. And I'll see her again tomorrow."

We stare at each other.

Say something normal. Say something normal. Say something normal. "So your Christmas song is killing it."

7

The Christmas song she just released is going absolutely bananas. It's trending on every chart a song can trend on. You can't open a social media app without the first ten videos you see all using parts of the song. I was in New York last week, and the billboard in Times Square was playing parts of the video every time I looked at it from my hotel room.

She shrugs. "Yeah."

Clearly not the right thing to say, though I don't know why. "You're doing Christmas with Cooper and Waverly?"

"Uh-huh."

Something's off.

Not that I know her well—we've only been in Malibu together at the same time maybe a month total—but now that it's just the two of us, things are weird.

I should leave her alone.

I should.

"You play darts?" I ask instead.

She glances at the board. "The last time I threw something at a wall, you had to get your roof fixed."

Not wrong, but it wasn't her fault. She was bouncing a rubber ball against the wall while working on some lyrics, and the ball went through the drywall. It had been quietly rotting for months due to a leak that wasn't obvious.

Not saying I made a big deal about sticking true to my humble roots and helping patch the wall when the contractors came by to work on it, but I'm not saying I didn't either.

I pluck the darts off the board and separate them to hand her the green darts. "Wanna see if Beck's walls have structural damage?"

"Absolutely not."

"You'd be doing him a favor. He's not out here often, so it'd be good for him to know if he has problems with his walls."

I get a half smile, and once again, I tell myself I should retreat.

I'm not blocking her in the corner, but I *am* her landlord.

And I know she had a lot of trouble with landlords before she moved in to my pool house.

Does she think I'm trying to hit on her and she has to tolerate it or find a new place to live?

I'm about to step back and let her go, but she reaches out and accepts the darts. "Okay, but if this goes through the wall and lands outside, you're telling Beck it was your idea."

"Deal. You know the rules?"

"Hit the dart board and don't put it through the wall." She's completely straight-faced.

It's fucking adorable.

I gesture to the board. "Ladies first."

"Am I back far enough?"

"Yep."

Not even close.

But if we back up much farther, we'll trip over other people.

She takes aim and lets the dart fly, and it *thunks* off the wall to the left of the target.

"That's seven points for creativity," I tell her.

Bad idea.

Bad, bad idea.

My joke makes her purse those curvy lips as she suppresses a smile, and it's hot as hell.

Stop it, I order myself as she takes aim with her second dart.

It misses.

So does her third dart.

"Forty-eight points for consistency," I say.

She cocks her hip to one side and gives me the look I've come to think of as her *this old weirdo has no chance with me* look. "I can handle losing."

"Who says you're losing? Maybe it's less about hitting the bull's-eye and more about seeing who can be most creative." I toss my first dart and miss on the other side.

On purpose. Of course I can hit a dart board.

"Four points," she says. "It would've been ten, but your dart had no good dismount off the wall."

"Huh." I aim my second dart, which hits the frame then flips a few times on its way back at us. It lands at Aspen's feet, stuck in the rug.

She looks at the dart, then up at me. "Did you do that on purpose?"

"Aw, you think I have mad dart skills."

"Do it again."

If she were one of my brothers or my sister or my friends from childhood and we were playing a made-up point game, I'd demand she tell me how many points I got first.

But I don't really care how many points this is worth in the game.

Not when I can show off my skills while she's half smiling, half suspicious.

"Hard shot," I tell her. "I'm not very good."

God, she's pretty when her eyes sparkle like that. "Throw the dart, Cash."

Know the last time a woman made me nervous?

Probably my ill-advised, ten-day-long marriage back in the height of my Bro Code days.

When I was about Aspen's age.

But I'm squinting in concentration as I aim for the dart board, looking for the same spot that I hit a moment ago.

I let the dart go, and *yesssss*.

It bounces off the frame again, flips in the air, and while it doesn't land quite at Aspen's feet this time, she still claps her hands and throws her head back with a laugh. "You did *not* just do—oh, fuuuu—crap."

She's staring at the ceiling.

I glance up too.

Hear a snicker behind me that could've come from any of my siblings or buddies or their siblings.

"Huh." My pulse ticks higher. I stretch my fingers out and close them into a fist in my suddenly clammy hands. Have to swallow against the sudden dry mouth.

We're standing under a massive ball of mistletoe.

It's not the only mistletoe in the room either.

See again, this place was decorated by an inebriated elf.

But it's the mistletoe that we're standing under.

Levi's kissing his wife under another ball of mistletoe by the stairs. Beck just snagged Sarah beneath some mistletoe in the corner I was just standing in with Davis.

"Mistletoe time!" my sister crows.

Fuck.

The kissing has to be done.

I swallow again and look down at Aspen.

She's staring at me. But is she staring at me like there are rules, and then there are *rules*, and this rule of kissing someone under the mistletoe must be obeyed regardless of who you're standing there with? Or is she staring at me like *this dude better not try anything?*

Not just my pulse inching higher now.

My dick is as well.

Her eyes dip to my lips.

I tell my cock she's staring at my nose and contemplating logistics. Kinda known for having a big schnoz.

My cock—and my brain—don't believe me.

She's staring at my mouth.

Her eyes dart back to mine. She bites her plump lower lip.

"There's—" My voice cracks. I clear my throat and try again. "There's this thing here where if you don't play by the rules, you're in danger of being the target of pranks for the next year."

"Huh."

That's it.

That's all she says.

Just *huh.*

Her gaze shifts from my mouth to my eyes, then back to my mouth.

I swallow again.

"I have seen what Cooper can do," she murmurs.

One time.

I can kiss this woman *one time*, using mistletoe as an

excuse, and then I'm buying a new house in LA to stay at when I'm in California and moving on from this crush.

So she can keep renting my pool house as long as she wants.

And I won't go fix anything that's wrong myself the next time something breaks. I'll have my people handle it for me.

Yep.

One kiss.

That's all.

I angle my body toward hers, hyper-aware of the way her eyes dilate, her sharp but soft inhalation as her gaze dips to my mouth again, her lips parting.

My hand settles on her waist as the sound of her viral Christmas song fills the room.

I start to smile, but Aspen—

She jerks back.

Completely closed up.

No more smiles. No more curiosity. No more *anything*.

"Fun game," she says. "Thanks."

And then she's gone, dashing through the crowd of my family and best friends, disappearing down the steps to the basement.

Fuck.

Way to go, creepy old guy.

Way to go.

2

Aspen Bowen, aka a rising pop star who's always been let down by the holidays

COME *to Virginia and have Christmas with Cooper and me,* my mentor and work bestie Waverly said three weeks ago. *It's low stress. Low expectations. Plus, daily pastries from his brother's bakery, and if you get tired of us, you can hide in a different part of the house.*

She gets not liking the holidays. Has her own reasons for it. Likes them better now that she's with Cooper.

But for everything Waverly's done in her career, she's never had a viral holiday hit about *forgetting Christmas* that she couldn't go anywhere without hearing over and over and over again when forgetting Christmas is exactly what she wants to do.

So last night, after my song started playing at the holiday party, I made my excuses about needing my own whole entire house for my holiday trip. Now I'm solo for the rest of the season, all checked in to a vacation rental cabin that feels miles and miles from civilization. There's another little town no more than ten minutes away down a winding mountain road, but I have everything I need here.

Food. Notebook. Guitar.

I wish I had Commander Crumpet too, but he's clearly happy with his new family.

And that matters more than what I want.

Especially since I have to move again when I get back to LA.

I know better than to flirt with my landlord.

I do.

I blame the stress of being under the watchful eye of the creepy elves that Beck and Sarah Ryder had on their shelves.

Temporary insanity making me give in to the idea that the movie star I've been crushing on for longer than I care to admit would see me as anything more than the hot mess who keeps breaking things in his pool house.

And then when I thought he was going to kiss me under the mistletoe—but no.

Nope.

The universe had other plans, and those plans were to blare my song and ruin the moment.

Which is good.

I can't buy a house until royalties come in for this dumb song, so I shouldn't be kissing my landlord until I have a more secure place to go.

But I push all of that out of my brain, settle onto the plush rug in front of the empty fireplace in the little wood cabin, and tune out the world while I fiddle with lyrics and a melody that I've been working on for my next album. Soak in the sound of a gentle rain that starts to fall midafternoon. Switch on a lamp that illuminates the log walls in a soft yellow glow. Debate starting a fire in the fireplace for more ambiance.

Get distracted by the idea of ambiance and go back to my journal.

At least, until I hear a car outside near dusk.

I'm at the end of a dirt road. The closest other cabin that I saw on my drive in this morning was much farther down the mountain. There's no other access to this cabin and nothing else *but* this cabin at the end of the road.

I angle myself off the floor, grunting as I realize my body's gotten stiff from sitting so long, and peer out the dirty window.

Maybe it's a cleaning crew here on the wrong day. Or the owner of the cabin. Possibly even someone like me who got double-booked, because wouldn't that be exactly how this holiday is supposed to go?

But no. Instead, I'm gaping, convinced my eyes are playing tricks on me.

Am I dreaming?

Did I fall asleep on the floor and this isn't real?

I push up off my knees, my lower back groaning.

Definitely not a dream.

But *what the hell* is he doing here?

Cash Rivers has three siblings, two parents, and dozens of besties to spend his holidays with.

Is this his stunt double?

No, I've heard his stunt double always wears a prosthetic nose, and why would a stunt double wear that off-hours?

Also, while I've never met his stunt double, I doubt a stunt double would make my heart race and send tingles through my chest the way Cash does.

It's so dumb.

I shouldn't like him.

I don't *want* to like him.

I want to spend a few years diving deeper into my career so I can know that when it all falls apart—and it eventually will, because everything does—I've been smart with my money and I can take some time to figure out what my next step in life will be *without* having to work three jobs to avoid moving into another apartment or rental with questionable landlords.

Cash is heading quickly through the thickening rain toward the cabin door. Eyes down on his phone but moving with that innate grace that comes with staying in shape for all of the action-adventure movies he does.

His light brown hair isn't as tame as it was last night, like he's been running his hands through it, and despite the temperatures hovering near freezing outside, his black jacket is unzipped, showing off the gray shirt underneath clinging to his pecs.

All of him getting splattered with raindrops.

I limp to the door like I'm forty years older than I actually am. Waverly keeps telling me that my posture will come back to haunt me before long. She might be right.

She'd be more right if she'd tell me to quit shipping myself with the older guys.

Cash is lifting his hand to knock on the door when I

swing it open. A blast of cold air and a smattering of icy mist hits me in the chest.

"What are you doing here?" I ask.

He shoves his hands in his pockets, glances at me, then down at the ground, then back up at me. "I'm sorry."

"For being here?"

"No, I *came* here to say I'm sorry."

The cold air has nothing on the panic that suddenly floods my veins.

Years of bad living situations are the only explanation for the next words out of my mouth. "You're kicking me out?"

"What? No. How could I—no." The utter confusion making his forehead wrinkle and his eyes squint would be cute if I were in a position to let myself actively think of him as cute.

Oh.

Right.

Who drives an hour out of their way just to tell someone she's getting evicted?

No one.

Probably.

My life is weird sometimes.

Cash scuffs his boot on the top step, his brown eyes darting over my face. "I won't ever kick you out. Promise."

Half of me swoons with this ridiculous crush.

The other half is focused on the weirdness of him being here. "You came to say sorry for what then?"

His lips part as he stares at me.

Apparently what he's here for should be obvious.

"Oh my god, did something happen to Commander Crumpet?"

"No."

"Waverly. Is Waverly okay?"

"No. Yes. Yes, Waverly's fine."

I'm baffled.

He's apparently baffled that I'm baffled.

We're a baffle sandwich, except we're the bread in the sandwich and the doorway between us is the filling.

"So you're sorry because…?" I prompt.

Also, why are men more attractive to me when they're bewildered and confused?

"I—I came to apologize." There's a level of uncertainty in his voice that does nothing to combat how adorable I think he is.

"I got that part. For what?"

"For…" He lifts his eyes to mine. Visibly swallows. "For scaring you away from the party."

His answer filters through my brain like it has to get through the outer layers of sludge and lyrics before it can hit the parts that understand what he's talking about.

But finally—

The kiss.

He's apologizing for looking like he was going to kiss me under the mistletoe.

Heat flashes across my face as the first drops of a freezing rain splatter the dead leaves littering the forest floor around the cabin behind him.

I wanted him to kiss me.

I was ready for him to kiss me.

Even knowing that he's a massive playboy, that the

gossip pages are always one step away from labeling him a *manwhore*, that kissing him would mean I'd once again have to move, there were multiple parts of me ready for him to kiss me.

I assumed he was willing to do it because it was expected when you're standing under the mistletoe, and that he didn't give it another thought.

The fact that he did—my stomach dips.

And then I take back control of myself. "You didn't scare me away."

"I—the mistletoe—and the rules—and I—when you bolted, I thought I'd crossed a line and ruined your vacation. Your Christmas."

Not *I wanted to kiss you*.

Nope.

I thought I ruined your Christmas because there was a rule about mistletoe.

I swallow hard against disappointment that has no right to be there. *He kisses women all the time, Aspen. You're not special.*

But he *does* care about me on some level. We're friends. Basically since the first minute we started texting about his pool house, I've felt we were friends.

And he's just reminded me that that's all we'll ever be.

"You weren't inappropriate last night," I tell him. "But stalking me out to a cabin in the woods…"

He looks up at the sky, up at the falling rain that's hitting him on the head, then blinks and winces, rubbing his eye like Mother Nature nailed him as he looks back at me. "I just didn't want you to think you had to run away instead of enjoying your holiday with Waverly. I tried to text you, but it bounced. So I tried to call you, and it wouldn't go through. I thought—I thought you blocked me."

I shake my head. "Glitchy cell signal here."

"Yeah, I—" He cuts himself off as another blast of wind blows the fat, cold drops of rain onto both of us.

I shiver.

He shivers.

Something beyond him creaks and groans.

His brows furrow together as he turns to look behind him.

I glance the same direction as the sound intensifies, and then I watch in disbelief as a large pine tree crashes to the ground just beyond where our cars are parked.

No.

No no no.

That didn't just happen.

The pine branches wave in the wind as the tree settles itself more firmly across the edge of the driveway, blocking the road.

"Oh, fuck," Cash whispers.

I look at his car.

It's a hatchback. No monster truck wheels that'll go climbing over a downed tree.

My rental is a Kia coupe.

It's not climbing a downed tree either.

The wind blows again, sending another blast of ice droplets at my face and chest.

Making a decision I'll likely regret, I open the door wider. Like I have a choice now. "Come in. Get out of the weather. I'll see if I can reach the owners."

He studies me warily. "You're not mad?"

"About anything that happened at the party? No." Conflicted about having him here right now? Yes.

I like Cash.

Cannot deny it.

I also know better for so many reasons, and I won't let being attracted to him derail any of my life plans.

Been there, done that. My hormones don't control my life. I control my hormones.

"But you're mad that I'm here," he says.

"If you're not going to come inside, you should leave, though I have no idea how. Pick one. I'm closing the door in ten seconds."

He doesn't answer immediately.

"Nine…eight…"

"Which do you want me to do?"

I want him to come in.

And I want him to leave so I can keep hiding from the world in peace.

Hence I'm making him decide what to do. "Five…four…"

He makes a soft noise somewhere between a growl and a grunt, and then he steps into the doorway. "If you want me to leave—"

And make him hike down off the mountain? There's no way his car is fitting between the trees along the side of the road, and it's certainly not going over the tree now blocking the road. "I'll say so."

I shut the door behind him and shiver again.

It's cold out there, and the rain is coming harder, *ping ping ping*-ing against the roof.

Everything about the cabin feels warm and secure.

I don't think we're in danger of roof leaks.

I hope.

Buildings and I don't always have the best luck.

But lately, Cash has always been around to fix what's broken.

Not that I couldn't figure it out if I had to. I've just been so busy with touring, writing, recording, avoiding the sound of my own voice singing about wanting to forget Christmas but falling in love over the holidays instead...

And I like it when he comes over.

It's dumb. I know he looks at me like a young performer to mentor. He's been in a band. He's an actor now. He knows more about my life than I probably do, so helping me out is paying it forward.

Plus, in the time I've lived in his pool house, he's been publicly linked to at least four different girlfriends. And that's only what I've noticed when I've looked at the gossip pages.

There have been weeks at a time when I couldn't be bothered.

"Cozy," Cash says as he glances around, pausing in the middle of the room, hands still in his pockets.

It *is* cozy. The log walls, the art prints of forest scenes, the jade-and-amber patterned rug, the brown faux leather sectional separating the living room from the small kitchen area, the stone fireplace and mantle, the windows framing the fireplace that look out over the pine forest up here, with the brown curtains featuring cute little bears— it's perfect.

For a solo *get back to center* retreat.

I pick up my phone and settle into the deep cushions of the L-shaped couch opposite the fireplace. "I got lucky."

"Just booked it today?"

"Yeah."

"Staying long?"

"Ten days."

"By yourself?"

"Yeah."

"If I didn't scare you away—"

"You didn't."

"I thought you were staying with Waverly for the holidays."

"Plans changed."

"You two have a fight?"

"What? No. Absolutely not."

"I'll be in the city for the holidays. Won't bother you a bit if you wanted to keep your original plans."

I lift my head from the message I'm typing out to the owners about how to clear a tree from the driveway. "Oh my god, *it wasn't about you.*"

He stares at me.

I stare right back.

He hasn't shaved. He has light brown scruff coating his chin and jaw and upper lip, and he looks like he belongs in a movie where he's the reluctant hero who has to save us all from an alien invasion.

I would watch the crap out of that movie.

"So why did you leave the party yesterday?" he asks.

Because nice holidays and I don't get along, and being by myself is safer. "I do weird things sometimes."

He gives me the eyebrow tilt of *I don't believe you.*

And here's the thing.

This could be Cash Rivers's ego—*of course you leaving was about me*—or it could be observant friend Cash Rivers —*you can trust me. Haven't all of our text message conversations this past year taught you anything?*

Either way, all he's getting is what I'm telling him now.

"I felt like writing songs, and I do it best when I don't have distractions."

Yeah, that's a total lie.

The part about feeling like writing songs, anyway.

What's weird though, is that I think he knows I'm feeding him a line.

He shouldn't.

We don't know each other that well.

Correction: we *shouldn't* know each other that well.

But between the mountains of texts we send each other and the vibe when we're in the same place, it feels like we know each other that well.

And that's what sucks about being his tenant.

If I were one more up-and-coming entertainer, I could absolutely bang this out with him.

But he's my landlord.

And he's also my friend.

I don't want to mess up either.

"You just suddenly needed to be alone and write songs?" he says.

"Yes."

"Okay."

Release a Christmas album, my manager said. *It'll remind people you're here while we work on your next album.*

Twelve songs.

Eleven written by other artists and licensed.

One written by me in a moment of weakness early this year when holiday decorations were still up everywhere and I'd just surrendered my pet to a better home and broken up with a guy who was using me for my connections to Waverly.

And that's the one song I can't stop hearing.

The one where I wrote myself a happy ending to the holidays.

Which has never happened in my twenty-four years on this earth.

A heavy gust of wind rattles the windows and throws thick raindrops against the glass.

We both look outside.

"Did you check the weather before you came up here?" I ask him.

"Light rain predicted. It should pass."

"Soon?"

"Couple hours at most."

I picked up enough food at the store to get me through two or three days, but when my song came on the grocery store speakers, I noped out of grabbing anything else.

I'm in that weird space where my career is taking off, but I can still go to the grocery store and not get recognized. Waverly flips out occasionally when I tell her some of the things I've done and places I've gone solo, but I like it.

And I know the next few months—or possibly even the next couple days—will determine if I'm ever able to go to the grocery store on my own again. On top of not wanting to hear my own song, I don't want to get recognized.

"Great," I say. "Once the owners get up here with a chainsaw, the weather will have passed, and you can spend your holidays guilt-free, knowing that you did nothing wrong."

Cash looks at my guitar, then at the fireplace, ignoring my comment about not feeling guilty. "You know how to build a fire?"

"Cooper showed me how at their house once last winter, and I'm apparently a pyromaniac at heart because I beg to do it anytime we're together somewhere with a fireplace."

"Got enough food and everything?"

"There's a shop about ten or fifteen minutes away."

Another massive gust of wind rattles the window, and the raindrops hitting the glass take on a new sound.

An icy sound.

Crap.

Crap crap crap.

If this is a *light rain*, I don't want to know what a heavy rain or an icy rain is.

"You're really okay here?" he says.

"Totally fine. I *am* a fully grown adult. It's a thing that happens with time."

"You lived near LA your whole life?"

"Mostly."

He glances at the window beside the fireplace again.

Wind howls over the chimney.

Dammmmmmmittttt. I hit *send* on the message, then put my phone down again. "Owners have been notified. They

27

were quick to respond when I couldn't get the key code to work earlier, so I'm sure they'll be quick again, and we can get you on your way home first thing in the morning."

He nods. Glances at the empty fireplace again. "You really want to be alone for the holidays?"

"The holidays and I have a toxic relationship."

That gets his attention. "What kind of toxic relationship?"

"Family members dying, breakups, years with no presents." I shrug like I don't hate this time of year to the depths of my soul. And like that's all it is. I might be fudging some of this. "The usual."

He takes a seat on the other part of the sofa, hands dangling over his knees, watching me. "So no Christmas decorations out here for you, huh?"

I shake my head as images of broken glass ornaments and a toppled tree and mashed potatoes dripping down the rose-wallpapered dining room wall at my grandmother's house filter through my brain.

That's the part I never talk to anyone about.

I probably should, but I don't currently want to.

There's a quilt that I found in the small linen closet with faded spring colors and a butterfly pattern. Looks homemade, but also like it's been washed a million times.

Like someone made it with love, and it's safe and cozy and won't bring up old memories that I'd rather forget. Unlike one of the other quilts with a Christmas pattern.

I grab the butterfly quilt and drape it over my lap, then reach for my journal too.

"You're really good out here?" Cash asks.

I nod.

"And you're not mad at me?"

I shake my head.

After a long moment of studying me, he nods too. "Okay. Sorry to bother you."

"You're not bothering me."

He grins that stupid handsome grin that could win him every last movie role in the entire world. "But you don't want me here."

"I mean…"

"It's okay. I get it."

Both of us look at the windows as another gust of wind hits the cabin.

Honestly?

Not my favorite weather.

I like being safe and warm in the cabin, but I don't like the way the wind and the rain sound.

It's ominous.

Or possibly I'm merely prepared for something to always go wrong during the holidays.

He eyes me, opens his mouth, then shakes his head and looks down at his hands.

His question about me growing up in LA was pointed. Pointed in the *you're not used to weather in colder climates* way.

"Sorry. Again," he says quietly. "For—misunderstanding."

"No worries." I tuck my feet tighter under the quilt. "It's kind of you to worry."

This isn't how we behave together.

We usually give each other crap. Him about me breaking his pool house, me about how he can't fix anything with his shirt on. Sometimes me about him looking cheesy in one of his movies, or him asking if I wrote a specific song as an homage to the traffic in LA.

Ever since the first text I sent him to ask if I could rent his pool house, we've kept in regular communication.

Like we're friends.

Or old entertainment industry insider and newbie learning the ropes.

We definitely talk more about our jobs than we ever do about who we might be dating or when we're seeing our family members next.

Or not seeing them.

But I wanted to be alone for the holidays. With the wind howling harder, the rain pelting the cabin harder, the temperatures *so* cold, and night falling quickly, I know there's very little chance that, even when the owners respond, they'll be getting up here to clear that tree off the road soon.

Cash will be spending the entire night.

It's fine though.

Totally fine.

He can have the couch. I'll take the bedroom. Tomorrow morning, the owners will show up, clear the tree off the driveway, and he'll leave.

And then I have another week and a half before I have to head back to the real world.

Hopefully by then, my life will be back to normal.

Hopefully.

3

Cash

WAY TO GO, me.

Good job impulsively chasing a twenty-four-year-old woman out to a mountain cabin when she's here not because of you at all.

You're doing a fantastic job of convincing yourself that you're not a creeper.

And now you're stuck here at least until morning.

The wind outside is the kind that causes trees to come down. *More* trees. The temperature's dropping fast enough that the rain will likely be sheets of ice within the next thirty minutes, which was *not* in the forecast.

And Aspen's curled up in the corner of the couch, pretending I'm not here while she scribbles in her journal, occasionally checking her phone and making the *they haven't replied yet* noise.

She's tried calling the after-hours number a few times, but none of her calls went through.

Apparently the internet is strong enough for email, but not strong enough for phone calls.

And now it's just the two of us.

Sitting out a storm and waiting for an email.

Ever feel like you're breathing too loudly?

That's me right now.

I'm breathing too loudly.

The last time I worried I was breathing too loudly was when I was probably seventeen or eighteen, hiding in a closet to spy on my sister and her first boyfriend.

Much different situation than being here with Aspen, occasionally hearing her pen scratch across the paper as the storm beats down on the cabin.

She slides a look at me. "Would you rather I go to the other room?"

The bad thing about always being busy is that you don't know what to do with yourself when you're not busy.

I'm not busy.

I can't get a cell signal.

The WiFi's flaky, which honestly isn't too surprising given the remoteness here and the weather.

I'd like to have the powers I had in a movie I did a few years ago where I could control the weather so that I can get out of her hair, except that was a fantasy movie, and I'm honestly only human.

And I know exactly how many people would bring me back to life to murder me for dying if I were to try to get back down off this mountain in this weather right now.

If I could get the car around the tree.

Which didn't look possible during the quick trip I took out to examine it during a short break in the rain a little while ago.

I'm well and truly blocked in here.

I shake my head at Aspen. "No. No, it's your cabin. I'm sorry I'm bothering you."

"It's fine."

It's not *fine*.

I'm way in the wrong here. I shouldn't have come.

I shove up from the sectional, positioned in the room to face both the fireplace, which is framed by windows, and the wall with the television, and head behind her to the kitchenette and dining nook. Nice little table here.

I can scroll my phone and see if I have enough WiFi power to download the script my agent sent me last week.

And I can hope this storm passes quicker than the few hours of rain that were forecasted.

But *rain* and *ice* are two different things.

If I'd known there would be ice, I wouldn't have—

No, that's not true.

If I'd known there would be ice, I would've grabbed more food than what I have out in the car, and that I'm now not so sure about bringing in to share with her.

Not with some of the things she's implied about the holidays.

What did she do last year?

I wouldn't know. I was here, seeing friends and family in Copper Valley, the way I have every year since the guys and I left home as Bro Code.

She twists to peer at me. "Why are we being awkward and weird?"

Because I thought it was necessary to stalk her to apologize for something that she apparently didn't even realize happened because she will never look at me as anything other than *that old actor dude who rents out his pool house to me.*

"I shouldn't be here."

"Well, you *are*, and we can't change that at this exact moment, so can we just be normal?"

Normal is me hoping she doesn't realize I sit on the balcony off my bedroom on the rare occasions that we're both in LA and she's playing her guitar and testing lyrics.

Normal is me getting excited when something breaks in the pool house so that I have an excuse to go in there and check it out, whether she's home or not, to see what new element of herself she's added. A mug with a funny saying here. A digital picture frame featuring mostly nature images mixed with the occasional shot of her performing somewhere.

Normal is the two of us texting late into the night, trading stories of being on the road for a musician's life, making me realize how much I miss it.

Miss it enough that I've started messing around with my old guitar again too.

I nod to her. "Yeah. Normal. This is normal." This is not anywhere near normal. And I'd appreciate it if the wind would quit howling outside. "You hungry? Want me to make you something?"

"I'm fine. Thanks though."

Yep.

Awkward as fuck.

I'd say I wish I stayed back at Beck's place or gone back into the city with my siblings, but I like being around Aspen too much to truly wish that.

"You need more water?" I ask. "Something else to drink? Levi always wanted tea when he was writing songs."

"Sure. Tea sounds nice. Thank you."

Aaaawwwwkkkkkwwwwaaaarrrd.

I'm the betting type, and I'm betting she's saying yes for the sake of giving me something to do. Not because she wants tea.

"Lemon? Honey?"

"Don't have any. Plain is fine. Thank you."

My stomach grumbles.

She looks at it.

I pretend it didn't happen and suppress another need to apologize for being here.

Normal days aren't full of *I'm sorry*s for me. They're full of working on a set, calls with my agent or business manager, and being catered to by half the people I come into contact with. I use my manners because, despite my age, my mother would murder me if I didn't. That will never change, regardless of how old I get or if she's still living or merely haunting me. But I do recognize that I'm catered to.

Not often my stomach grumbling doesn't result in someone handing me a sandwich.

Especially not while I'm being as quiet as possible in hunting down a teakettle and a mug.

But it's not just about this moment.

It's about me being stupid enough to come up here without taking into account that a couple hundred feet in elevation can be the difference between the rainstorm that the town's likely getting, as expected, and the ice that's pelting the cabin up here on the side of the mountain.

And then arrogant enough to wonder how she'd fare by herself if something happened like the power going out.

As though she's not an adult and this place isn't stocked with firewood and blankets.

"The tea's in that black cloth bag by the fridge," she says. "I brought plenty. Help yourself if you want some too."

I dig into the bag and find there's not a lot in it.

Cinnamon graham crackers. Three bananas. A bag of mandarins. Another bag of carrots. And a carton of lemon raspberry tea bags. "Is this all of your food for the week?"

"There's more in the fridge."

I take a peek.

One block of cheese, a pint-size container of almond milk, and a pack of chicken breasts.

I look at her.

She's gone back to scribbling in her journal. But she still mutters, "It'll get me through a few days."

"No judgment. Eat what you like. Girl dinner, right?" This storm will pass. The cabin's owners will get the tree cleared away. She'll be able to get more food.

"I had a bigger list, but they were playing my song at the grocery store."

"You get recognized?"

She shakes her head.

"Gonna happen pretty soon."

"I know."

"Probably need to think about—"

"Not while I'm in a cabin in the woods."

Security. A business manager or executive assistant to travel with her. Probably a publicist and stylist too.

People.

That's what I was going to say, and she knows it.

For the moment, she's right. Support staff and a security team aren't necessary in a secluded cabin in the woods. Hell, I didn't bring any with me myself, and I do tend to have a whole team most places I go.

With the way her career is going, she'll need them soon too.

"How big is the store?" I ask.

That has her turning around to look at me again. "You are *not* getting me groceries. You *will* be recognized."

"I don't just play action heroes in the movies. I also have slick skills with navigating small grocery stores too fast for the local gossips to arrive and corner me."

"Hello, ego."

I grin. "Well-earned. Even if they try something, look at these guns." I flex my left biceps.

"Nice padding in that jacket you've got on."

My favorite thing about Aspen?

She gives me shit. Regularly.

It's like we've been friends for half my life, despite the fact that I was practically old enough to have a driver's license when she was born. By the time she was old enough to get a driver's license, I'd already had a successful career in a boy band and had moved on to a second career in Hollywood.

"It's all-natural padding," I say.

"Wool? Or cotton?"

I'm grinning broader as I fill the teakettle with water out of the sink. "Meat. All meat."

"Chicken or beef?" She's smiling too.

"Grade A top sirloin. With a space. Sir. Space. Loin."

"If you have to explain the joke…"

"You're still laughing."

"Pity laugh."

"Liar."

"I just don't want you to feel bad about yourself."

"You can use that in one of your lyrics. No attribution necessary."

"*I just don't want you to feel bad about yourself,*" she sings.

"*I am grade A top sir space loin,*" I sing back.

She blinks at me. "Oh my god. I forgot you can sing."

"Probably because you were still in diapers when I was hot."

Fuuuuck.

Her eyes almost cross with the acrobatics her facial muscles are doing, and then the most beautiful but also terrible thing happens.

She busts out laughing.

She has the prettiest laugh. It fuels fantasies I refuse to admit to even myself most of the time.

But also, she's laughing at me being an old man.

While her giggles peter out and she goes back to her journal, I set the teakettle on the stove and flip on the burner, then dig into the cabinet for the best mug.

The first one I spot says *World's Greatest Grandpa.*

Fantastic.

Even the cabin is mocking me.

What I get for talking her address out of Waverly and coming up here in a fucking ice storm to check on a woman who was *fine* by herself.

I settle on a mug that has a cartoon dog on it, with *Don't bone breaking my heart* written on it, then move around the kitchenette, being nosy.

Been a few years since I was in a vacation rental. Or possibly many, many years. Especially one-bedroom, log-walled vacation rental cabins that don't come with a personal chef and an on-site cleaning crew.

I should come to places like this more often.

It's cozy.

Quiet.

Smells like cedar and rosewater. Like my grandma's sitting room.

She was a badass. Left home at sixteen to pursue a career as an actress, lied to everyone about her age, fell in love with my grandpa—who was ten years older than she was—and moved across the country with him to Copper Valley to raise babies and help lead the high school's drama program.

Lied about her qualifications there as well, but no one cared.

She put on good shows.

I miss her.

Aspen gives me the same vibes. Fearless. Bold. Determined.

I overheard Waverly say once that when her team

reached out to Aspen, Aspen's initial response was basically *you can't fool me, assholes.*

My grandmother absolutely would've said the same. *Why would someone on top of the world want to talk to me? You can't fool me with your shenanigans, whoever you are.*

I finish Aspen's tea and carry it to her in the living room, then retreat to the kitchen and pretend I'm reading something on my phone.

What I'm really doing is watching her.

She blows on the tea before sipping it. Sets it on the half-barrel end table beside her, then goes back to her journal, occasionally bopping her head or lifting her chin like she's looking to the ceiling for an answer.

"What rhymes with tomato?" she says suddenly.

I almost drop my phone in a rush to answer. "Space potato."

"Something not food."

"Purple Play-Doh."

"No, something in nature...like..."

"Tornado," I say at the same time she says, "Volcano."

She frowns at me. "I might like tornado better."

"Why are you writing lyrics with tomato in them?"

"That's for me to know and you to be hella impressed by when my next album drops."

"Ah. You don't believe fully in the tomato yet."

"If that's what you need to tell yourself..."

"*I* believe that you can make the tomato work. I just don't think *you* think you can make the tomato work."

Another gust of wind shakes the cabin, and we look at the front windows.

Full darkness surrounds us, so all there is to see is the

two of us staring back at ourselves like the window is a mirror.

But the *plink plink plink* against the glass tells me what I already knew.

We're headed into ice storm territory.

If that's the case, I'm not leaving in the morning. Even if the tree gets cleared away. Which is feeling less and less probable by the moment.

And given all of that, it's also unlikely that I'm sleeping at all tonight either.

4

Aspen

I RETREAT to the bedroom shortly after nine and spend a couple hours attempting to binge a television series I want to catch up on. The cabin's WiFi works so-so with my phone, so it's a glitchy binge-watch, but I manage to mostly enjoy it.

No messages from the owners.

And it's getting later and later.

But I can't fall asleep.

Drifting off is absolutely impossible.

It's not the wind. It's not the sound of the heavy, icy rain pounding on the roof. I'm not too cold. Not too hot. The mattress is surprisingly plush and comfortable. The scent of cedar throughout the house is pleasant and soothing.

This should be the perfect place to sleep.

But when Cash so much as *thinks* of moving out in the living room, I hear it.

Swear I do.

Every time I tense, thinking he's moving, I hear confirmation moments later. A deeper inhale, a shuffle of fabric against the fake leather on the sectional, a glass clinking as it's set down on a solid surface like he needed a drink in the middle of the night.

Morning takes forever to arrive.

And when it does, the first rays of sunlight show that we have bigger problems.

I have bigger problems.

The entire world is a fuzzy sheet of white.

Cash is right. I'm a California girl, and a warm-weather SoCal girl at that.

But even I've seen enough of the world to recognize that neither of us is going anywhere when I can barely see the trees around the cabin through the swirling wall of snow. I can only tell where the tree that fell yesterday is sitting because the snow pile on top of it is uneven and lumpy, whereas it's a pristine white sheet everywhere else.

And it means one thing.

He's stuck here with me.

I don't get my alone time.

I whimper in utter frustration, and almost immediately my spidey senses tingle. A moment later, he calls, "Aspen? You okay?" in a deep, raspy morning voice that makes my nipples tingle.

"Stop it," I whisper to them.

There's a shuffle outside my door, and the primitive

part of my brain wonders if he'll have bedhead and be in a wrinkled T-shirt.

Great time for my libido to betray me.

"I'm fine," I say.

The shuffling outside the bedroom stops. "You need anything?"

Just to shove the inappropriate attraction to my landlord back into the box where it belongs. "I thought I packed my favorite yoga pants and I didn't. I'm fine. I'll find some way to survive this tragedy."

"You want to borrow mine?"

I suck in a surprised breath and choke on a dust particle, which sends me into a fit of choking laughter.

"Men can wear yoga pants too," he says through the doorway, which makes me laugh and cough harder.

His voice gets closer. "The only reason I'm not breaking this door down to make sure you're alive is because I can hear you breathing."

"*Breathing?*" I wheeze out.

I'm not *breathing*.

I'm choking and laughing so loudly, they can probably hear me at the next cabin, which is at the bottom of the long, windy road up this mountain.

"Making noise," Cash says. "Breathing. Same thing where I grew up."

"Short of weird smells or a serial killer vibe, there's no reason for you to assume something horrible happened while I was sleeping." I pull myself together, grab a pair of sweatpants and a baggy hoody, slip them on, and then open the bedroom door.

Cash is leaning against the opposite wall, just outside

the door to the lone bathroom. His eyes go alert and wary at the same time as he sweeps a quick glance up and down, like he's making sure I survived the night.

He's still in his jeans from yesterday, naturally. Not like he planned on staying or needing a change of clothes. His gray T-shirt is wrinkled but still clinging to his broad chest and solid biceps, and his brown hair is all kinds of messy.

Why is he so hot?

Sincerely. Why?

Why does he have those thick veins wrapped around his forearms?

Why are his nipples poking his shirt and highlighting how solid his movie-star physique is?

Why does looking at him make my lungs tingle?

We don't kiss our landlords. Bad things happen when we kiss our landlords. Ask me how I know.

But I've never had a landlord who would've driven an hour in the wrong direction for his holiday plans to apologize for anything. And *especially* to apologize for something that didn't even happen.

"Sleep okay?" he says.

"Absolutely," I lie. "You?"

"Like a baby," he lies right back.

It's not just that I spent the night listening to him moving here and there. It's the dark smudges under his eyes, the dip of his lips, the sag of his shoulders.

Either he's one of those people who wake up slowly, or he slept like crap.

"So, I was on the WiFi." He doesn't just look tired as he says it.

No, he looks guilty.

"Were you streaming porn?"

"*No.*"

"Then why do you look like you using the WiFi is the worst thing you could've done?"

He cringes and looks at the floor. "I pulled up the weather."

My heart thuds against my ribs. "And?" I ask, like I don't know on some level what he's about to say.

"Blizzard developed unexpectedly and isn't over until late tonight," he mutters.

"Blizzard?"

"Couple feet of snow should fall before it's over."

I stare at him.

He scuffs one socked foot against the knotted wood floor. "Good news is, I have more food out in my car. I'll head out and grab it before the snow gets any thicker."

"And the bad news is, you're not leaving."

"Yeah."

"Sorry. I didn't mean that to sound—"

"No, you wanted to be alone. I'm intruding. I get it. It's hard enough to find alone time with the way we—*you* live, and I shouldn't be here."

But he is here.

There's a part of me that doesn't mind. When Waverly found out that my latest apartment wasn't working out well, she insisted on helping me find a place she knew I'd be comfortable, and the next thing I knew, *Cash fucking Rivers* was texting me about renting his pool house.

There was definitely some freaking out going on. I'd once joked to her that I should date Davis Remington to increase my visibility in the world by bringing him out of hiding and making a big splash, but I never imagined she'd hook me up with another former Bro Code member to live with.

It was definitely an *I'm out of my league* moment.

But our conversations quickly turned easy and friendly, like we'd known each other forever.

On one level, he's my friend.

And then we met in person, months after I moved into his pool house, and everything changed.

At least for me.

I started having dreams about him. *Weird* dreams, but good dreams. Dreams where he was kissing me. Talking dirty to me. Telling me I was his designated sex partner for alien explorations. Sometimes he'd strip me out of my trench coat in the middle of a mall that was actually a nursing home, and then we'd have sex in the food court while the elderly pet store employees rated our performance, which squicked me out because *ew*, but also, in my dreams, Cash Rivers is exceptionally good at giving me orgasms.

And then I wrote "Forget Christmas."

My anthem about hating everything about the holidays…until *he* arrives.

About *him* showing me the magic of the season.

I've told absolutely no one that Cash was my muse. Not only am I a hot mess of a rising pop star who breaks things in every house, condo, apartment, or spare room that I move into, but I'm also too busy for relationships.

Besides, he sees me as a little girl who needs guidance, and he's promised his friends he'd watch over me.

If life has taught me anything, it's that you put your energy toward the practical and possible.

It's still astonishing to me that having a career as a singer-songwriter *is* possible, but it is.

The other thing life has taught me is to accept kindnesses when they come your way.

Waverly is that kindness.

And if all of this—the songs, the albums, the *viral sensation*, the tours and performances—if it all goes away, *I will be okay.*

But if I let myself love someone and they don't love me back, I won't.

I left that behind the minute I turned eighteen and moved out of my parents' house.

No one will *ever* break me like that again.

No matter how handsome and charming and sexy he is.

And that's probably why I've broken up with every man I've ever dated. I don't have it in me to be the level of vulnerable you have to be in order to have a relationship.

I straighten my spine and look him dead in the eye. "We should probably get that food out of your car before it gets harder to get to your car."

The number of times he's winced or cringed in the four minutes that we've been talking is a bad sign.

"What?" I say.

"You…aren't a fan of the holidays."

"So?"

"In my defense, I was working with what I had and historical knowledge of other women in my life, and I didn't know you didn't like the holidays. Also, you were at a holiday party, and you looked like you were having fun."

How can I not appreciate this man? He seriously needs to go before I do something stupid. Because he's freaking adorable right now. "Is it food?" I ask.

"It'll give us calories when your food runs out."

When your food runs out.

Oh, no.

Oh, no no no. We're not doing *food running out* at the holidays.

Been there, done that, and I am *not* signing up for it again. Even if there are no decorations, no music, no *A Christmas Story* on repeat on the television for days, no yelling about how someone needs to turn off that goddamn annoying movie, no pity cookies dropped off from the neighbors, I'll still know it's the holidays.

"Cash?"

The man refuses to look me in the eye while his face does a thing that I loosely translate to mean *I don't want to tell you more bad news.*

"How long will we be stuck here?"

He mumbles something.

"*Cash.*"

He answers the ceiling instead of me. "Given how remote it is here, it could be a week before we can get plowed out. Partially depends on whatever arrangements the cabin owners have for the driveway."

"I'll email them again."

He gives me another look.

"What?"

"It was a couple hours ago that I had enough WiFi to

get the weather. Haven't been able to get it to work since. Cell signal is nonexistent. I've been trying to get a message out to my assistant to get help up here sooner since I checked the weather, and it won't go. I'll go get the extra food."

I grab my phone and pull up my email, which takes forever to connect, then sputters out immediately. I trail him out to the living room. "I'll help get the food."

He puts a foot into one boot. "You have a warm coat?"

"It's just ten feet."

"Snow boots?"

I open my mouth, then shut it again as I eyeball the boots he's also eyeballing next to his.

Mine are ankle-high purple suede with a heel.

While his boots are also ankle-high, they look like hiking boots. Not like something that would bring all of the fashionable squirrels to the yard.

"Might take me a couple trips," he says. "Stay at the door. You can take everything inside while I go back out for more."

It would be quicker and more efficient if both of us went out to the cars, but my version of being prepared for a snowy mountain Christmas was to not have to go anywhere, and I packed accordingly. Plus, it's not like I have a full winter wardrobe.

"Can you grab a thing or two out of my car too?"

"Yep. Keys?"

I fish them out of my bag and hand them to him. "There's a gallon of water and a backpack with some books. Be careful."

"It's not war, Mabel. It's the future of the entire planet," he replies.

And I laugh.

I actually laugh. "That was the absolute worst movie you ever did."

He winks. "Yet you still watched it and recognize the line."

My god, he's handsome.

Does he know it?

Does he know exactly how attractive he is?

I tell myself he probably does. The idea that he's full of himself makes it easier to remember that relationships are trouble, and crushing on your landlord is always a bad idea.

He slips out the door.

I close it behind him, and then I dash to the window to peek out and watch him.

Merely because it's so thick with falling snow that I can barely see the cars.

This is me watching for his safety.

Not me watching his ass as he braves the weather to bring in a few more supplies.

Yep.

Just watching for his safety.

And I need to get a lot better at lying to myself.

5

Cash

FUCK ME, it's slippery as hell out here.

There's a layer of ice beneath the rapidly accumulating snow, and I almost wipe out before I get off the two steps leading down to the parking area. A snowflake blows into my eye. Wind cuts through my gloves.

But I'm all in on this mission.

We don't have enough food, and it'll only be harder to get back out here later, when there's more snow.

Need to get to the extra firewood on the side of the cabin and bring more of that in too.

Don't let Aspen know how precarious this could get if the power goes out.

Which wouldn't be surprising, given the wind and the snow.

We're at the end of the grid. Before this is over, I

expect there will be many downed trees and houses without power.

The door opens behind me before I get to my car. I turn back and spot Aspen through the thick, blowing snow. She's only in her oversize hoodie and thick sweatpants.

"What are you doing?" I ask.

"I got into the original email from when I booked the place," she replies. "The owners say that in the event of snow, there's a shovel in the small shed out back, and that they'll eventually get up here to get us plowed out. They said there's extra firewood on the side of the house if we need it too."

"Good job. Get back inside."

The door clicks shut behind me again.

And then I reach my car.

Fuck me six times over.

My door's open.

My fucking car door is open.

Which means—

"Why is your door already open?" Aspen calls behind me.

"Get back in the house."

"I can't be inside when I can't see you through the window. The snow's too thick. What if you slip? What if a tree falls on you? What if aliens attack?"

I stare at my open car door.

It's my brother's Subaru. I could've borrowed my other brother's Porsche, but I wanted something suited for mountain roads.

And now I'm feeling like the biggest dumbass in the history of dumbasses.

Don't leave food in your car in the mountains.

"Cash?" Aspen says.

"Get back inside," I repeat. "I think a bear went through the car last night."

"*A bear?*"

"It's fine. It's gone."

"Are you sure?"

I angle a look inside the back seat, where I had piles of gingerbread house kits and bulk store bags of truffles and hot chocolate and more, and yeah.

Yeah, there was definitely a bear here.

Everything's scattered and ripped open, chocolate smearing the seats, ripped cardboard and half-pieces of gingerbread houses littering the footwell along with the snow gathering as it blows into the car's interior. The other door's open too, like the bear climbed through.

Shit shit shit.

I trudge through the thickening layer of snow to Aspen's rental.

No bear damage to her car, at least.

But it's iced over, which means it takes work to get the trunk open because I'm fighting a sheet of frozen water.

Once I'm in though, it takes no more than a few seconds to grab the water jug and her backpack. No extra bags of food in her car. No extra blankets. Not even a roadside emergency kit. It's the brand-new kind of clean and empty.

"Aren't bears supposed to be hibernating?" Aspen calls.

"Would you *please* get back in the house?"

"Not if a bear's coming back to eat you."

"The bear had a feast in my back seat. He's not coming back to eat anything. *Get inside.*"

"If the bear's supposed to be hibernating and went through your car, then a bear could come back to eat you."

She has her arms wrapped around herself and her hood pulled up and cinched tight around her face so that all I can see are her eyeballs, nose, and half her mouth. And it's hard to see that much through the swirling snow.

I pick my way back to her and hand her the frozen gallon of water and the bulky backpack. "Please put this inside."

"Where are you going?"

"See what I can salvage."

She huffs, sending a puff of white into the air. She's utterly adorable in this moment. Especially with the way the thick snowflakes are accumulating on her dark brown eyelashes and all over the top of her black hoodie.

"Cash. It's freezing out here. A bear ate everything. I'm a pop star. We don't eat. You're a movie star. You don't eat. We're fine. Just get inside too."

I open the door and gently shove her. "Four more minutes. I'm fine. Please go put this inside."

"If a bear eats you—one, you deserve it for being stupid, and two, I'll never forgive you for adding this to my holiday trauma."

Fuuuuck. "There's no bear to eat me."

"There was a bear here in the past twelve hours. How do you know it's not lying in wait to—"

I clamp a hand over her mouth, which I should absolutely not do, because now soft Aspen breath is blowing through my gloves and into my palm and prompting me to fantasize about touching her silky skin. Her hazel eyes widen as she locks gazes with me, and *dammit*, I want to kiss her.

I want to kiss her so badly that my bones ache with it.

And that's not the cold talking.

It's not the situation.

It's her.

It's always been her.

"There's no more bear." My voice is strained from holding back this desperate need to wrap her in my arms, carry her inside, wrap us both together in a blanket, and kiss her until I can't breathe. "I'm salvaging food. Back in four minutes. Go inside."

She stares at me with bright, unblinking hazel eyes for an eternity where I don't feel the cold, don't see the snow, don't hear the crack of a tree falling somewhere nearby.

And then she makes another little noise and ducks back into the cabin.

It shouldn't be possible to have a boner when the weather's this cold, but here I am, striding back toward my car, my feet slipping, my cock hard as a damn rock.

All because I touched her.

I shouldn't be here.

And now I'm stuck.

For days.

With the one woman I cannot stop thinking about and absolutely cannot have, with limited food and no way of getting out.

I find two tins of those twirly stick cookies, an entire stollen cake, and one bag of boozy truffles untouched. They go into a bag from the back end, where I find an intact gingerbread house kit too.

If it weren't snowing so hard that I can barely see the house, I'd clean out the mess so the bear doesn't get back in the car.

My brother will never let me live this down.

As he shouldn't.

When I turn toward the house, I spot Aspen on the step outside the door again. "What are you doing?" I call to her.

"Watching you in case you fall," she replies.

"I'm not going to—"

I don't finish the statement.

Why?

Because I'm suddenly flat on my back, the cloth bag whipping around to smack me in the face.

Thanks, ice.

Thank you so much.

"Oh my god," Aspen gasps.

"*Stay*," I wheeze out.

My entire body is going to hurt tomorrow.

And I'll probably have a welt in the middle of my forehead too.

I force myself upright, sitting in the snow in my jeans, and reach for the scattered food.

"Cash—" Aspen starts, but I cut her off.

"*Stay*," I repeat.

My lungs burn. My ass aches. Shoulders too.

But I make myself rise as Aspen ignores my order and

skitters down the steps in those damn purple boots that likely have zero traction.

"It's icy," I tell her. "Don't—"

"C'mon," she says, holding out a hand. "Up you go. And then neither one of us is going outside again unless we absolutely have to."

I glance at the woodpile, barely visible at the side of the house.

We're going to have to leave. And also hope the extra wood isn't too wet to burn. Got a feeling we'll need it.

I don't want to freak her out, but this situation is going to get worse before it gets better. And I need to get inside and get prepped for it.

"You should've stayed in the house," I grumble as I climb to my feet all on my own.

I don't want to pull her down.

It's slick as hell out here.

"You too," she replies.

We make it the rest of the way inside in silence.

It's not far.

Maybe ten feet.

But it feels a hundred times longer.

I'm cold. My jeans are wet. I don't have anything to change into.

If I'd stayed away, she'd be inside, still sleeping. She'd be warm and dry and happy. Having nice dreams and waking up and having her holiday time off her own way.

Instead, we're both shivering by the time we get inside.

The door's been opened a half-dozen times, and I don't think it's just the effect of the chill outside making the living room feel colder. It's possible the heater can't keep up.

We're in a bad spot.

I need to start a fire.

Get out of my pants and dry them.

And make this even more awkward than it already is.

6

Aspen

WHAT DO I want to do right now?

To hide in the bedroom and rest or journal or stream a show if the internet will hold up enough for it, which it clearly won't today. We're completely internet-less.

But what do I also want to do?

Be near Cash, who has steadfastly refused to take off his wet pants in the time since he got back inside.

I want to fill these containers with water.

Why?

Probably on a well and the power might go out, which will mean no water.

That was definitely *not* in the listing for this place.

Or in the email from the owners about procedures in case of snow.

And then—*why are you going back outside?*

Better to get more wood in to dry now in case the power goes out. No power means no heat.

So he went back outside, *in the freezing cold*, to get wood to stack just inside the back door.

Shaking off the snow and ice log by log before he set it in the house.

Which brings us to now.

"Why are men so flipping stubborn?" I ask him as he kneels in front of the fireplace, blowing on the embers coming off the burning newspaper that he's using to try to start the fire now that he's apparently satisfied that we're ready for an apocalypse. "I can start a fire. You don't have to do all of this."

"I'm not stubborn. I'm efficient. And unlike some people, I know how to start a fire with something other than a blowtorch."

While I snort like he's not absolutely right that half the reason I like starting fires at Cooper's place is that he lets me use his small blowtorch to ignite the wood, Cash blows on the smoldering newspaper again. This time, one of the smaller sticks catches on fire. The embers beneath it glow red, and soon, more sticks are catching, leading to the big log catching too.

He doesn't leave it alone until the fire's roaring, then he puts the screen in place on the hearth.

"Can you *please* get out of your wet pants now?" I ask.

And let me inspect your booboos.

The way he landed on the ground looked like it hurt, and I've seen him wince a few times while he's been running around prepping us for Armageddon.

I don't care how many of his action movies I've seen

where his character pushes through the pain. It hurts, and he could probably use—something.

Ice.

Heat.

Painkillers.

A massage.

From me.

While he's naked in front of the fire.

Stop it, Aspen.

He's staring at me as I sit wrapped in a quilt on the sectional, but if he knows what I'm thinking about his pants, he doesn't let on.

Just nods once. "Yeah. Good idea."

Like I haven't said it six times already. Like it's only just *now* a good idea.

He grabs the top quilt out of the linen closet and heads to the bathroom.

Moments later, he emerges with the quilt wrapped around his waist, looking like he's Father Christmas from ye olden days, if Father Christmas also wore tight gray shirts over his holiday robes.

His pants get laid out on the floor near the fire, which is making the room warmer—almost too warm—with every passing minute.

I'm glad we're both safe and sound in here now. Not slipping on ice. Not worrying about wildlife. Not in blinding snow so thick you can barely see ten feet past the door.

It's time for me to go hide in the bedroom.

Definitely time.

Yep.

This is me, going right now.

Getting up off the couch.

Walking down the short hallway.

Closing myself in—

Okay, seriously, I'm not doing any of that. I'm tucking my feet under me and wrapping my quilt tighter around myself too. I'm still using the butterfly quilt.

I like it.

I asked before, but I need to ask again. "How long do you think we'll actually be stuck out here?"

"Few days for sure," he says. "Maybe not a full week. Not if the owners have someone lined up to plow and clear that tree."

"Will your family worry?" With the internet out, neither of us has been able to reach anyone we know.

He shakes his head. Then nods. Then sighs. "They know where I was going. Is it weird to say I might get a helicopter lift once the storm blows over?"

"Yes."

The man smiles.

So damn gorgeous.

"Tell you a secret?" he says.

I nod.

"Ten-year-old me would think that's fucking awesome."

"I don't know many people at many ages that would take a helicopter rescue from a snowed-in cabin for granted and not think it's awesome on some level."

He huffs out a *heh* laugh. "Good point."

"Nice to have friends who can afford a helicopter *and* still like you enough to come for you."

He's smiling as he glances at me. "Who's worrying about you?"

Isn't that the question? My manager would probably worry. My agent. The producer Waverly introduced me to for my next album who's been absolutely amazing. And I do have a few friends in LA that I check in with regularly.

But they all have their own traditions with their own families this time of the year, and I told them all I'd be with Waverly. "Anyone who would've needed me knew I'd be off-grid through the holidays, so probably no one."

His brown-eyed gaze doesn't waver. "Who'd you spend the holidays with last year?"

"Commander Crumpet."

He watches me, his smile dipping away.

I turn my attention to the fire.

If it weren't for the slight panic at the possibility that we'll be trapped here for more days than we have enough food for, this would be nice.

Is there any better place to write out all of your frustrations and fears and hopes and dreams while scribbling lyrics and chords than in front of a fireplace in a snowy mountain cabin?

I could fall asleep here. Wake up, journal some, work some, and take another nap to compensate for not sleeping last night.

Naps have been in short supply in my life this past year. Not that I wanted or needed them before, but I've also never been this busy, even when I was working two or three jobs to stay afloat.

There's more pressure here. More stress. Bigger stakes with more people involved than have ever been involved in my life before. And I like those people. They've been incredibly kind.

But I'll see them again *after* the holidays.

Not now.

This cabin should've been exactly what I needed to rest, recuperate, connect with nature, and get back to my budding career, refreshed and ready in the new year.

Instead, I'm battling a lingering fear that we don't have what we need to make it through this snowstorm.

And it doesn't matter how much money either one of us has in our bank accounts.

Not when we can't even get a text message out.

We really might be at the mercy of his friends and family realizing they can't reach him and trying to get a helicopter up here when the storm blows over.

That's beyond fathomable. Especially to ten-year-old me who learned the hard way over and over again that you can't depend on people and you can't count on miracles either.

Which suddenly makes me wonder if my career is real. My friendship with Waverly. My music—my escape, my love, my joy—paying my bills.

How long it will last.

What will ruin it.

"Is there any chance the bear will break into the cabin?" I whisper.

Cash scoots closer to me on the couch. Not close enough to touch, but closer. "No."

"How do you know?"

"Bears avoid humans. But if it makes you feel better, I'll shove furniture in front of both of the doors."

"And the windows?"

"They're too lazy to try to climb through a window. Besides, it got everything it needed last night."

"You're an expert on anonymous bears' eating habits?"

"It wasn't hungry enough to eat everything in the car."

Oh.

That makes some kind of logical sense. "Did it get into my rental too?"

"Nope. Yours is fine. Just mine. Probably have to buy my brother a new car now though."

I stare at him for a moment, fully digest what he's just said, and then, despite myself, I start laughing.

We're stranded in a cabin, miles from civilization, in a snowstorm on top of an ice storm, where a bear broke into his car last night, with no idea how long we'll be unable to get out, and he's cracking jokes about buying his brother a new car.

"It's his," he adds. "And the bear's worse than some of the kids he's nannied for. Bigger fingerprints. More capacity to toss shit everywhere."

It shouldn't be this funny.

Is this what it feels like when you laugh because you're panicking? Or is it actually that funny?

"Is it that bad inside the car?"

"Probably worse."

His deadpan delivery makes me laugh harder.

He drops his voice to a conspiratorial whisper. "But that's not even the worst part."

"What is?"

I'm anticipating him telling me the bear relieved itself all over the car.

That's not at all where he goes though.

"The worst part is that all of the food came from Beck's place. I cleaned him out of every last bag or box of Christmas food that he had stashed to get him through until New Year's."

"*Why?*"

"I didn't know you hated the holidays, thought apology food was necessary and themed apology food was better. Not like I can hit the warehouse store by myself a week before Christmas. I would've been mobbed. So I took Beck's stash. Dude eats like it's his full-time job. He's gonna be so pissed."

I don't know if he's being completely serious or merely acting completely serious, but it's working.

For a split second, I'm convinced that the very worst part of our situation is that his friend, the rich-as-sin former-boy-bander-turned-underwear-model, will have to send his housekeeper or assistant to the store to get more red-and-green Hershey's Kisses so he doesn't starve to death.

And that makes me laugh even harder.

Cash glances at me again, smiles a soft smile, and shakes his head before looking back at the fire while I let myself giggle through the half panic, half gratitude, until I can breathe normally again.

Finally, I suck in a big breath, then let it out while my shoulders sag.

"Better?" he asks.

I squeeze his arm, ignoring his tight muscles and the way my palm tingles from touching him. "I'm glad you're here."

"You shouldn't be."

"I can build a fire. Even a fire that doesn't start with a blowtorch. I can figure out how to use a snow shovel. I can live for a week on three chicken breasts and a bag of mandarins, but...I'm glad I'm not alone."

"You don't have to say that. Especially since you don't have much of a choice."

"I'm a fighter," I tell him. "I'm a survivor. I'd be okay. I'd figure out what I needed to figure out. And I'm very, very grateful right now that I don't have to survive on my own. Thank you. For being here. And being my friend."

He keeps staring at the fire, a muscle in his jaw ticking behind the scruff growing over his chin and cheeks.

"And I'm sorry you got stuck," I add quietly.

He likes the holidays. He doesn't see his family often.

He's missing his time with them, and that feels wrong.

His voice is even softer than mine when he says, "I'm not."

Hello, Mr. Overprotective.

That kind of sentiment from a man usually makes me twitch. I've had to take care of myself for so long that I get triggered at the idea that someone else thinks they need to take care of me. Especially since most of the men who've claimed they want to take care of me have let me down one way or another.

But I don't tense or get irritated when Cash does it.

Probably because we made friends over text before we really got to know each other in person. I'd met him at a party at his Malibu mansion a few months before I needed a new living situation, but it was obvious when I messaged him about renting his pool house that he didn't remember who I was, so it was like starting over.

Waverly told me later she hadn't reached out herself the way I thought she had. She'd run into Beck Ryder while she was celebrating the Fireballs' World Series win with Cooper, and their conversation turned to me, and when Waverly mentioned I'd just had a highly uncomfortable situation with a landlord and had moved into a hotel but needed more stability and better security than a hotel could offer, Beck said he knew a guy with a pool house that was set up like an apartment.

She didn't realize he was talking about Cash until after I'd moved in.

And then she'd laughed and laughed and said it was a good thing I'd be traveling a lot.

He has parties all the time, she told me. *You'd never get any rest if you were both always home regularly.*

Not surprising. I met him the first time at one of his parties. The gossip pages call him the Hollywood Heartbreaker. Always hosting or crashing a party. Different model or actress or singer on his arm at every red carpet. Unless he takes his mom or sister.

That's why they love him so much. Because in addition to always being seen with a new *It Girl*, he also raves about how much he adores his mom or confesses that he wanted to make his sister's day by introducing her to some of her favorite people who are definitely *not* him.

Just like when I'm thinking I've ruined his Christmas, he goes all *I'm glad I was here for you so you didn't have to do this alone.*

"I would've been okay," I repeat. "I always am."

He grunts a nonanswer response.

I should go back to the bedroom.

I should.

But I don't want to.

Even as an awkward silence falls between us, I don't want to.

However, that's where my journal is.

And I'm not here to secretly fawn over my landlord.

"So, anyway, I need to get some stuff done." I untangle myself from the quilt and rise.

He nods.

That's it.

Just nods.

He doesn't say *sorry I crashed your getaway* again, but I can feel the apology hanging in the air between us anyway.

I pause before slipping down the short hallway to the bedroom. "When I come back, can we be normal again?"

His gaze snaps to mine. "Yeah. Of course."

So not normal.

Not at all.

I stifle a sigh.

This is going to be a long, long storm.

7

Cash

EVERY TIME I think I'm bored, I remind myself it could be worse.

The power has held for hours even if the internet is completely dead.

The snow's probably two feet thick already. Other than seeing Aspen for a few brief minutes when she came out to get a mandarin and a hunk of cheese for lunch, I've been left to entertain myself.

I find a book on a shelf under the television, but it doesn't hold my interest.

I shuffle through the cabinets and find a weird mix of dry goods and spices.

TV gets a few channels that seem to be coming from a satellite dish, but even that is cutting in and out. Every time a show stalls, I give it a few minutes while I lapse into the dozing kind of sleep and try again.

All. Day. Long.

While Aspen's in the next room.

Sometimes I hear her humming. Then there's strumming on her guitar, often with the same chords repeated while she works something out.

When she's not playing, she mutters to herself every once in a while too.

Usually the same time the television loses signal.

She probably has a television in the bedroom too.

Once my pants are dry, which takes most of the day, I use the shovel to clear a path to our cars just to have something to do. When I step back inside, Aspen's in the kitchen, poking around in the cabinets.

I shut the door behind me and shrug out of my coat. "There's pancake mix in the cabinet."

She looks down at my crotch. "Did you get your pants wet again?"

Dammit. They're soaked. And also, there's a little more *dammit* that she's not eyeballing the goods.

Don't be an inappropriate creeper, asshole.

I toe my first boot off. "Nah. Maybe a little. I'll rotisserie myself in front of the fire and be fine. Good day?"

"Yep."

This is not normal. I feel like such an intruder right now. "You feel like pancakes?"

She pushes up on her tiptoes, shoves some things around in the open cabinet, and goes flat-footed again as she pulls out a jar of sprinkles. "Only if they're fun pancakes."

I kick off my other boot and pad into the kitchen to join her.

"You cook?" she asks me.

"My mom taught us all how to cook as soon we turned ten, and she'd raise holy hell any time any of us boys tried to get June to cook for us."

"But do you still know how to cook?"

"Pretty sure I can handle pancakes."

Her eyes sparkle as she grins at me. "Guess we'll see then, won't we?"

While I take over in the kitchen, gathering ingredients and setting a pan on the stove to heat up, she pulls out a bottle of wine from a box under the table.

"Where'd that come from?"

"Waverly and Cooper's collection."

Huh. Didn't know Cooper was a wine guy.

"He's not," Aspen says as if she's reading my mind. "I mean, he's not anti-wine. But Waverly's driving their collection. She started visiting wineries around all of the baseball cities when she was traveling with him last summer."

That's the part of being on the road I miss.

Seeing new things.

Exploring what makes each city unique.

The rest of the guys would sleep in on the bus or at the hotel, and I'd be up heading off to see a brewery or an art gallery or the world's biggest pencil, getting back in time for sound check or appearances at pet shelters or children's hospitals or whatever else our manager had lined up for us when we were on tour.

"I didn't steal the wine," Aspen says dryly.

I shake my head, realizing I'm frowning. "Didn't think you did."

"So what's with Mr. Grumpy Face?"

I rip open the bag of pancake mix and scoop a cup of it into a large bowl. "I miss it."

"Wine?"

"Being on the road."

She pauses with the cork halfway out of the bottle. "Are you serious?"

"I like new things. Checking out wineries at every stop sounds like fun."

"She had a blast. And I have a blast every time I see her get tipsy on wine now."

"You ever get to explore while you're on the road?"

She finishes uncorking the bottle and sets it aside before joining me briefly in the kitchen to grab a mug. "Not when I'm doing shows five nights a week. Maybe once I'm big enough to just do weekend shows, but not right now."

"Yeah, the early days are rough."

She dangles a second mug at me. "You want some?"

"No wine glasses?" I measure out the water and dump it into the mix, then go digging for something to stir it with.

"Even if there were, I'd rather drink my wine out of a mug that recognizes my awesomeness."

Ah. She's found the *classy as fuck* mug.

"Red or white?" I ask.

"Red."

"Like a bold red or a wussy red?"

She crosses the kitchen back to the table and the waiting wine bottle. "Like the only kind of red I have here."

"Aren't you supposed to have white with pancakes? Match the colors or something?"

"The sprinkles have red in them."

"That's like saying you have to have white wine with steak if it has a butter sauce on it."

"One, I take my steak plain and as close to raw as possible while not being refrigerator temperature on the very rare—heh—occasion that I can afford steak, and two, no wine for you if you're going to be picky about it."

Mental note: get her a steak dinner when we're out of this.

Other mental note: *don't be a fucking creeper.* "I'm not being picky. I'm being informed."

"Bottle's right here, bud. You can read the label yourself. I'm simply going to enjoy it for what it is, which is a wine that my friend thought I'd like."

Normal.

We have achieved normal.

Complete with me having fantasies about playing footsie beneath a black-clothed table at a fancy steak restaurant where her hair is swooped up and her eyes are sparkling and she's laughing at all of my jokes and reaching across the table to touch my hand with a promise of more touching to come—

Fuck me.

I turn my attention back to the task at hand and hit the pan with a sprinkling of water. It sizzles.

Pancake time. "Do you get tipsy on wine?" I ask her.

"Only when I want to."

I'm grinning, but it's short-lived.

I have pancake batter.

I remembered to put the sprinkles in.

I have a skillet.

I do not have butter.

And this skillet looks like it hasn't been nonstick since the 1980s.

Aspen takes her first sip from the mug, and a smile blossoms on her face.

She's so fucking pretty.

So pretty.

If she were ten years older, I'd be saying to hell with the pancakes and kissing her.

But she's not.

And I need to get my head on straight.

"This might not last, but I'm enjoying the hell out of it today," she murmurs as she swirls the mug and watches the wine inside.

I frown at her. "What might not last?"

"Try the cabinet next to the fridge," she says instead of answering me. She settles into a chair at the small table, crossing one leg over the other, and points with her wine mug. "I think I saw some olive oil in there. Not ideal, but it's better than crusty pancakes."

I go digging, and *yes*.

Even better than olive oil, there's nonstick spray.

Looks expired, but it's butter flavor. "Did you bring all of this?" I ask her as I get the first pancakes on.

She pauses with the mug halfway to her mouth. "You've never stayed in a vacation rental house, have you?"

"I might've once a decade or so ago."

Her smile explodes again. "You want to live, book

yourself a vacation rental once a month and see what weird things happen. Usually they're nothing out of the ordinary, and if they've been around a long time on the rental sites, you'll have stuff like the pancake mix that someone else left here. But sometimes you get in a situation with people who aren't authorized renting out a house, or with previous people leaving their edibles or mega boxes of condoms."

She takes another sip of wine, then continues. "And sometimes the houses are just strange. I stayed in this one just outside of Cleveland that had pink toilets and a massive marble statue of a vagina in the courtyard out back. But the house itself was built in like the early nineteen hundreds. There was zero water pressure and the beds were so soft that I couldn't sleep. Except for the bed in the attic room. That one was so hard you might as well have slept on the floor. And it smelled very weird."

"You always stay in vacation rental houses when you're on the road?"

"Depends on how long I'm in any given city."

"You have a favorite city?"

She opens her mouth to answer as I reach to flip the pancakes, and there's a massive *pop* that plunges us into darkness.

Fuck.

Aspen makes a noise as my eyes adjust to the low light coming off of the fire in the living room.

"You good?" I ask her.

"Did the power just go out?"

"Yep."

I pull out my phone and flip on the flashlight, taking care not to aim it at her.

"I mean, duh. Yes. Of course the power went out. Like you thought it would." Her voice is a little higher than normal.

"Happens in heavy snowstorms." *Cook, pancakes. Keep cooking.* Wonder if I can finish the rest of the batter over the fire? Also, is she panicking about the power being out? "We're as prepped as we can be. Nothing to worry about."

But don't flush the toilet. Or plan on taking a shower.

Also—*shit* again.

I head around to the window over the table, drop the blinds, and pull the curtains shut, then do the same in the living room and the bedroom.

When I leave the bedroom, I shut the door.

Aspen's still at the table when I get back to the kitchen and peek at the pancakes with the light from my phone.

Not quite cooked all the way through, and with the heat off, the pan's cooling rapidly.

"Aspen?" I say as I will the pancakes to keep cooking.

She shakes her head. "I'm good."

No, she's not.

Not with that tremble in her voice and her stiff posture and the way she's staring at her mug.

"We're gonna be okay." I abandon the pancakes to go squat in front of her, wanting to touch her and absolutely not daring to. "Lucky you, you're with a guy who's survived three apocalypses, two famines, and a few dozen alien invasions."

"You were *acting*."

"It felt real when you watched the movie though,

didn't it? Plus, one night at poker with the guys, I was being an ass about wiping the table with them, so they started reading all of the criticisms of *When Comes the End*, and I have been corrected on every basic survival skill that movie taught me. I've got this. *We've* got this."

She eyes me.

And it's not one of those *you have something on your face* looks.

It's *I don't know if I believe you* in her wary expression.

"We do. We've got this," I repeat.

She glances at her wine, then at me again. The shadows from the fire and my flashlight are making her look even more unsure, and that has my heart pounding.

I want her to believe in me.

It matters.

Even though I know it shouldn't, it does.

It's so damn hard to not touch her. "You said it yourself earlier. You would've made do on your own. You're fine."

"You've never yelled when I break stuff in your house," she says quietly, "so I don't expect you to yell now, but I'm not used to emergency situations where no one's yelling."

"Do you...want me...to yell?"

"No! No. I just—I expect it, and I don't like it, and it's not—it's not you, okay?" She huffs out a laugh that's not funny at all. "This is why I should've handled this alone."

Fuck it.

Just *fuck it.*

I lean forward and wrap her in a hug. "No yelling, I promise."

Her body shudders against mine. She drops her head to my shoulder. "Thank you."

Anything for you, Aspen. Fucking anything.

Her hair smells amazing, and I don't care that it's tickling my nose. I could hold her like this for eons.

But she tenses like she again knows what I'm thinking, and I drop my arms. "You want an almost-cooked pancake or three? Nothing like that hot runny batter surprise."

Another small, forced laugh slips out of her lips. "Sure. Thank you. Do I—can I do anything else to be prepared here?"

"Got water, got fire, got food that you can no longer see is holiday-themed. We're as good as we can be."

Except for the last part that I'm not telling her.

Can't hurt to hope for a miracle that gets the power back on in a matter of minutes or hours instead of potentially a couple days, can it?

8

Aspen

THANK GOD FOR THE WINE.

It's taking the edge off of my anxiety.

But not *quite* enough given what Cash is doing now.

Since having the almost-cooked pancakes, we've stuffed towels at the base of the doors to prevent drafty cold air from seeping in, debated if we should gather freshly fallen snow to melt for more water now that we've confirmed the power being out means no water as well, and now we're sitting in the living room by the fire, since it's the warmest part of the house and my fingers are cold.

Not that I told him my fingers are cold.

Not after that hug he gave me when I wanted to completely crawl into him and ask him to never let go.

I don't like being that vulnerable with anyone.

Even myself most of the time.

So since we're once again as prepared as we can be, I've sat here and sipped wine.

He's asked questions about my calendar once the holidays are over.

It got awkward again.

And now he's heading to my bedroom.

"What are you doing?" I ask him.

"Moving the mattress."

I think about it and realize I can't argue with his plan.

Nor do I want to. Even when the implications—*I'm getting our bed ready*—are making my nipples tight and my vagina excited.

Not gonna happen, I tell them.

They snicker back at me.

He's sleeping on the couch, I inform them. *He's getting the mattress, which he'll insist I use myself with half of the quilts while the fire keeps the whole room warm enough for both of us to sleep here without touching, because the man does not want to touch me.*

They're full-on guffawing now.

I ignore my horny body parts and make myself useful, picking up everything between the couch and the fireplace so that Cash can get the mattress down easily.

It's a double.

Not even a queen.

And he's carrying it like it's light as air.

Neither one of us says anything after he gets it placed on the floor near the fireplace.

We both stare at it for a long minute.

Then he mutters, "Pillows," and heads back to the bedroom.

I get to work straightening the sheets and making the bed. The bedroom door clicks, and a moment later, he sets the two pillows on the bed.

I shake out one quilt.

He grabs another.

We stand at opposite ends of the bed and take turns setting quilts out.

Not talking.

Once the bed's made, we both stare at it.

"I need to write some stuff down," I say at the same time he says, "I saw a book I'd like to try to read again."

We look at each other.

Then at the mattress.

He clears his throat and sits on the couch.

I grab my journal and plop down in the middle of the bed.

He uses his phone for a light for the book.

I use the fire for the light for my journal, which I'm not writing a damn thing in.

Would it be wrong to invite him to sit here with me? The couch has to be colder, and he's done so much work to get us ready to survive the night. He deserves to be closer to the fire.

If he wants to be.

Maybe his body temperature runs hot all the time.

Who knows?

He clears his throat again.

I glance over at him.

He nods at my journal. "You writing a book?"

"No. Lyrics. Poems. Gratitude. Trauma dumping. It's all-purpose without a plot."

He's quiet for a long minute while the fire crackles and I hold my pen over the pages, my brain continuing to be a blank slate.

While I'm poised with my pen, unable to move, he shifts on the couch.

Is he creeping closer? Is he cold? Is the fire not putting out enough heat?

"I keep one of those with me most of the time too," he says.

He is *definitely* closer. Very much sitting at the edge of the couch.

I shift like I'm adjusting my hips and inch a little more toward him too. "For lyrics, poems, gratitude, and trauma?"

"Yeah."

There's something hesitant in his voice.

Something that has me watching him as he stares at the fire, arms draped over his knees, book dangling from one hand. He's in his jacket and jeans again.

I flip my journal closed. "Did you write songs for Bro Code?"

One shoulder shrugs. "Levi and Davis did most of it. I'd help sometimes."

"Because they asked you to or because you wanted to?"

"Wanted to."

"You still write lyrics?"

"Chords and melodies and arrangements sometimes too."

His ears are turning pink.

It's adorable.

"I took violin lessons in grade school," he tells the fire.

"Then piano with Levi and Tripp when I got older, and I taught myself guitar when we started the band."

I'm picking up the same *I miss it* vibe that I got while he was making pancakes and talking about touring. I shift fully to face him, completely intrigued, all of our awkwardness forgotten.

"Are your songs good?"

"No."

His answer is so instantaneous that I don't believe him. "Is that insecurity or objectiveness speaking?"

He slides me a look.

Insecurity.

My heart squeezes. "Can I see?"

"Didn't bring it with me."

"I didn't mean *now*."

He grunts a nonanswer.

"What kind of songs?" I press.

"Bad songs."

"*Cash.*"

"It's nothing anyone's streaming these days."

I'm sure it's great isn't our normal. We give each other shit in person. We laugh. We joke. We don't go deep.

Deep only happens occasionally in text.

But neither of our phones will send messages right now, and even if they could, we need to conserve the battery power on both of them as long as we can.

He's already flipped off the flashlight on his phone since he's not reading.

And now I'm staring at him like I'm waiting for him to take it back.

Screw this.

I flip to a page in my notebook, scribble out *If you like it, someone else will too*, rip the page out, and thrust it at him. Texting won't work, but this will.

He takes it and stares at the note like he can't read it.

Or possibly like my handwriting is terrible.

Very well could be that.

But after a long moment, his lips quirk up on one side.

He leans close enough to me to pluck my pen out of my hand, sets the paper on his thigh, scribbles something himself, and hands me back the paper.

Or I'll burn all of my careers down in flames for taking such a wild left turn.

I roll my eyes.

He snatches the paper back and bends over it while he writes more, wrinkling the paper against his leg.

When he passes it back, our hands brush, sending a shiver up my forearm.

But when I read his note, a squeak of outrage slips out of my mouth.

I showed our old producer and he told me to keep my day job.

I grab the pen. *Fuck him*, I write back.

Cash snorts and takes the pen back from me.

A moment later, I have the most Cash Rivers answer I've ever seen, in or out of text message. *He wasn't my type, and even if he was, I hear he sucks in the sack.*

I snicker.

This time when I take the pen back, it's warm.

Like *he's been holding it* warm.

I have a problem if I'm getting tingly in my lady bits over holding a pen that he held.

Definitely should've been snowed in with someone else.

Except I don't think I'd be tolerating anyone else.

You should record the song and release it yourself, I write.

Songs, he writes back.

Excellent. Glad we're on the same page. I look forward to hearing your self-produced album.

He slides me a look as he's reading that last one.

Then he takes a long, *long* time to write out an answer.

And when he does, I swear my heart stops again.

I'm getting tired of the Hollywood networking grind. I miss touring. I miss being on a live stage. But if I went out on tour with a solo album, people would show up for the shit show of watching me be bad, not for the talent.

"Are you freaking serious?" I say, my voice weird and loud in the peaceful atmosphere that the crackling fire and low light are giving us.

He looks at the ceiling. "It's not *bad.* But it's not top-ten quality, and I know it."

"How about sometimes you do things just because you love them? Who cares how many people are watching from the audience if you're enjoying being on stage? Who cares how many records you sell if the joy was in making the record itself?"

His brown eyes flicker over my face. "You know you're fucking irresistible?"

My stomach collapses in on itself, my breasts tighten, and my vagina clenches while I try to not suck in a massive breath of surprise.

He scrubs a hand over his face. "Shit. Sorry. I didn't say that."

You're fucking irresistible.

He absolutely did too say it.

And it has my brain suddenly tripping over itself, trying to analyze what he means while my heart turns into a caffeinated squirrel.

I wish I could read his mind.

And it's not the first time I've wished I could read his mind.

We've been at his house at the same time for approximately three weeks over the last year, total. Despite how much we've texted, I likely haven't personally interacted with him more than a dozen times.

But sometimes I imagine he's looking at me the way I've seen Cooper look at Waverly. The way I've seen Levi Wilson, another former Bro Code member and currently a solo pop star on hiatus, look at his wife.

And that's why Levi's on hiatus.

For his wife and her three kids that he's taken as his own.

The idea that Cash would look at me like he cares is all in my imagination, and even if it wasn't, I don't need a relationship.

I'm too busy taking care of myself for a relationship.

"You think I'm irresistible?" *Shut up, Aspen. Shut. Up.*

He stares at the floor and mutters back, "How can you not know you're irresistible?"

My heart stops and my breath trips.

My brain tries to tell me that my ears heard him wrong, but they didn't.

I heard him right.

It's even more obvious when he says, louder, "I like you."

"No."

He half grins, then shakes his head.

And *oh my word.*

His cheeks are turning pink. Even when he's lit only by the orange glow of the fire, I can tell he's blushing.

My heart starts beating again, far more rapidly now. It's skipping through spring tulips.

"Yeah," he says. "I do. I like you. And I shouldn't—wouldn't—say it, but the fire is all we have aside from body heat to stay warm. So I owe it to you to tell you that I like you, and I'll do everything in my power to stay on this couch, but if survival instincts kick in, I might—get closer. And it might be uncomfortable, but I won't do anything intentionally inappropriate. I just...thought you should know."

This man—my friend—my mentor—my landlord—is sitting mere feet from me, hasn't had a drop of wine, and is telling me he likes me and we might have to snuggle to get through the next few days.

When I like him too, no matter how much I don't want to, because I still need a few months of a place to live before I have the cash in my bank account to buy myself a house.

Would it be awkward if I reached for my journal and started scribbling right now?

Probably.

Nearly definitely.

I like you too.

The words are on the tip of my tongue but I can't say them.

If I say them, it's real.

If it's real, he might try to kiss me like he did under the mistletoe two nights ago.

I might like it.

And then he leaves for his next movie shoot and I leave for my tour and we go back to texting like nothing happened, or worse, we don't text at all and I have to find another new place to live.

"I know." His voice is raw and husky in a way I've never heard in any of his movies. "I'm well aware I'm too old for you. I'm well aware it's probably awkward and weird for you to think about it. But I like you. I liked you when we were texting before we met in person. I like knowing you're safe in my pool house when you're in LA. I like sitting on my balcony listening to you write songs when I'm there too. I like when I get an excuse to come fix something. I just—like you. I keep trying not to, and I can't help myself."

My first boyfriend swore he'd rescue me and take me away from my shitty home, but when his mom heard, she made him break up with me.

The first boy I slept with ran for the hills when my period was late the next month. The first guy I moved in with was using me to get a job. I had a two-week thing with another guy whose biggest struggle in life was how he'd tell his parents he scratched up the BMW they gave him for his birthday. I called it off with him after he counted out to the penny how much I owed him for a dinner date he'd invited me to at a restaurant he knew I couldn't afford.

There haven't been a lot of people in my life who haven't let me down.

Honestly, even trusting Waverly is scary sometimes. The only reason I agreed to meet her in the first place was the logic that she had nothing to gain from helping me or being my friend. I can't make her richer. I can't make her more famous. I'm blunt and sometimes crass and I don't hold back.

And I've been around her enough now to recognize that she craves that in her life because she doesn't get my level of real many other places.

Cash gets realness from his family. I met all of them—his family, the friends he's tight with, the significant others who have joined their broader friend-family unit—at the party the other night.

I can't make him richer.

I can't make him more famous.

He has nothing to gain from liking me.

And he flat-out just said he shouldn't because he's *too old*.

But if the biggest thing I have to lose is one more place to live, then screw it. I can almost afford to buy a house myself.

So just *screw it*.

We're going there. And we're doing it now.

9

Cash

I SHOULDN'T HAVE SAID any of that.

Not a single word.

Hi, Aspen. We might have to cuddle naked and I will defi-nitely get a boner when we do, so I'm warning you about some-thing that might not actually happen if the power miraculously turns back on, or if the fire gives off enough heat for me to stay here on the couch.

Almost forty years on this earth and I am still an awkward dumbass when the cameras are off and I let myself be real.

She's fully facing me now, and I don't know what that look on her face means.

"Is this how you flirt with the models and actresses and performers you bring with you on the red carpet?" she asks.

Fuck.

There's no other word for this situation beyond *fuck*.

Most of them are only a few years older than Aspen.

"They're…picked on purpose," I tell the fire beyond her.

"It's all a ruse," she murmurs. "You do the Hollywood publicity game. Keep them talking about you by having a different woman at every event."

I tug on my collar. "Not all of them. Just…most of them."

Got an actress who needs some publicity before they announce she's starring in a big role, my agent will say. *Take her to your premiere, get seen walking out of Whole Foods together. Her people are tight with that director you've been wanting to work with.*

Showrunner was just announced for that book-to-movie adaptation you said you wanted to star in. They want a Casanova type. So-and-so from such-and-such modeling agency owes me a favor. Pack your bags. We're getting you a hot date to Fashion Week.

Big director on an action film is wooing that new rock chick. Take her to the charity event next week. We'll get you on his radar through her, and I'll find out what her team wants in return.

And so on.

It's all this-for-that. The game behind the scenes.

If we click right, we'll blow off steam in bed together, then go our separate ways. If we don't, we're professionals and treat the entire event that way.

"Do you ask how old they are before you agree to look like you're dating?" she asks.

I wince. "No."

"Then why does it matter how old I am?"

Fuck again.

This time because the question has my balls tightening and my cock getting hard.

I swallow.

Open my mouth.

Decide *because I see myself as your mentor and father figure* is the worst lie I could utter right now, and close my mouth again.

The truth is closer to *because I like you more than I like any of them.*

"How old did you think I was when we were texting?" she asks.

I look at the fire again, but it doesn't offer up any free passes. "I don't know. Late twenties? Mid-thirties?"

"You didn't look me up?"

I'm fish-mouthing again.

There are zero good answers to that question.

When Beck pinged me a year ago to ask if I'd consider renting my pool house to someone as a favor to a friend of a friend, I assumed he was talking about someone who'd been in the trenches trying to make a name for themselves for years.

Just talk to her, Beck said when I initially refused. *You get someone trusted to make sure your housekeeper isn't pulling more crap. She gets a place to live. You never have to see each other because she travels a lot too. Struggling musician type. I passed her your number. She'll use the code phrase 'Noses are red and your first wedding was a massive mistake' when she gets in touch.*

She did.

She used that exact phrase and followed it with *Also, if that's the code phrase your friends pick, I don't want to know what code phrases your enemies would use.*

We texted for hours.

I almost missed a flight.

I had my business manager do the paperwork for the pool house rental. She moved in while I was gone and texted me pictures of the plants around my pool to assure me they were still alive under her watch.

When I got back, she was traveling, so I texted her pictures of the pool house to show her it was still standing.

We texted other stuff too.

Long day shooting. This is a nice life, but sometimes it wears you out.

I was doing a set at this club in Boston and someone started throwing those weird gummy Nerds things at me.

Saw my family today for the first time in months. I always forget how much I miss them until I see them.

Must be nice—my hedgehog is basically my family. Well, and Waverly.

Waverly's name should've been a clue, but it wasn't, because I didn't pay attention to the young woman Waverly introduced me to one night at a party at my place several months before Beck pinged me.

Waverly and I weren't tight, so meeting Aspen was no more of a thing than meeting up-and-coming actresses at other parties around town. I registered meeting someone new, introduced by someone that I assumed worked the game the same as I did. I recognized our paths likely wouldn't cross again, or if they did, it would come with a formal introduction from my agent, and I moved on to hanging out with my inner circle.

I probably hit six parties that week.

It's what you do when you're in town for a few days and you're looking for what's next and you want to network and see a few friends.

Seven months into Aspen living in my pool house, we were finally both there at the same time. Ironic, considering I'd helped her find Commander Crumpet a new home without ever actually seeing her in person.

I was nervous as fucking hell to meet this woman that I was obsessed with.

Probably had three fake girlfriends in the time we'd been texting.

I hadn't hooked up with any of them because they didn't live up to what I imagined Aspen to be.

My hands were sweating. Mouth was dry. Dick and heart half clenched in terror that the vibe I got through texts wouldn't be the same vibe I'd get in person.

I was nervous to knock on the door of my own damn pool house.

But I did it.

And when she opened the door, soaking wet from her hair to her crop top to her baggy cotton shorts to her painted toenails, I almost choked on my own tongue before getting a word out.

"You're blonde," I'd blurted, barely stopping myself from saying *thirteen* and swapping it out for her hair color at the last possible second.

Pretty hazel eyes stared back at me with a deadass *I look like I just went for a dip in your pool with all of my clothes on, and you want to talk about my hair color?*

And the thought of her swimming in my pool—naked, to be completely honest, despite the fact that she was wearing clothes at the time—made my dick do things it definitely should not have done around *Waverly Sweet's best friend*, who couldn't have been more than twenty-four years old, and whom I finally recognized for who she actually was.

She asked me if I knew a good plumber because the dishwasher had just made a weird noise, and when she opened the door, the sprayers stayed on and soaked the entire kitchenette.

I got to play hero because I knew how to shut off the water line.

And then I went back inside my house and jerked off to images of her thanking me with her mouth on my cock.

Nothing has been right in my world since.

Including now, when Aspen's smirking at me, which isn't doing anything to relieve the pressure in my dick. "You thought I was some waitress who should've given up her dreams a decade or two ago."

"I thought you were someone with a lot more life experience."

"News flash, my friend. Some of us pack more life experience into every day than other people have to."

We've never talked about where we come from. Just where we are. But the little she's said on top of what she doesn't say is cluing me in to the fact that there's likely a reason she's never talked about where she used to live or what she used to do.

"And even if we don't," she adds, "age is just a number. It's only a fraction of who we are."

That sound?

That's not wind. It's not trees groaning under the weight of the snow outside. It's not either of our hearts beating or the fire crackling.

It's the sound of my brain catching up to the fact that she's telling me I'm not too old for her.

It's the sound of my cock catching up to the hint that she might be interested in me. "You don't care how old I am?"

"The second time we were both at your house at the same time, you had a party where you did shots off an ice luge and jumped into your pool with all of your clothes on. I think it's safe to say I don't look at you and think you were bound for the nursing home the next week."

I snort out a soft laugh. "I forgot about that."

"Because you're old."

"*Hey.*"

She cackles.

It's fucking delightful.

"I was trying to distract myself from following you around the party," I admit.

I shouldn't.

This is going nowhere.

But we're stuck. It's warm in front of the fire. And she's so damn pretty with her hair down—brown now, what she insists is nearly her natural color—her face free of makeup, wrapped in loungewear.

It feels like home here.

Like someplace I could spend every day and never get tired of it.

She pulls her legs up to her chest and lays her head on them, still wrapped in her quilt, watching me.

"I wrote 'Forget Christmas' about you," she whispers.

No.

No fucking way.

I scratch my chest, unable to reach where it's actually itching deep inside, under my breastbone, approximately where my heart is located.

"No, you didn't."

"I did. I didn't want to do a Christmas album. I didn't want to record twelve fucking songs about a holiday that's given me nothing but bad memories. So I asked myself what would make me happy, and your face popped into my head. Because you're my friend. And you're hot. And I just...wrote it like you made Christmas better."

"Aspen."

"The day you knocked on the pool house door and the dishwasher had just exploded—you didn't yell at me. I was sure you'd yell at me, and I was ready to yell right back, but you didn't blame me."

"You looked really good wet."

Her eyes smile. "When I broke your wall, you laughed. You *laughed*. And then you asked me what color I wanted the room when everything was fixed, like it was my house."

"You see it more than I do."

"I don't have permanent homes. I don't get comfortable. I don't break things without expecting a blowup. But you made me feel like I belonged because you wanted me to pick a paint color. I don't think you can understand how big that was."

She doesn't have family to spend the holidays with. While I don't know her full history, I know she's had several bad rental homes. Waverly is the only friend I've heard her talk about, and the only job she's mentioned prior to her pop career taking off was something to do with medical billing.

People have hurt her.

Not just *someone*.

Multiple someones.

I want to hunt down every one of them and make them pay for how they've hurt her.

She hugs her knees tighter. "Part of me is still waiting for you to decide you want your pool house back and that I have to go."

"It's yours as long as you want it."

Those wary eyes gut my soul.

Truth? I don't want her in my pool house.

I want her in my *house* house. In my kitchen. In my living room. In my bedroom. In my shower. Sprawled out on my dining room table.

Stop it, I order myself.

Doesn't work.

Not when she wrote a song—her most popular song—about me.

Not when I want to be the man standing between her and every bad thing that could ever happen to her from now on.

Not when being here with her is only making me want her in ways I've never wanted another woman.

That's why I tell myself I'm too old for her.

It's why I tell myself she sees me as nothing but a mentor.

Because if I give in, if I tell her how much I want her, if there's even a chance she wants me back—I can't fuck this up.

Not with her.

I like her too much for her to be one more woman I've screwed around with just for fun.

I don't want *fun*.

I want *everything*.

"This would be much easier if you weren't nice to me," she whispers.

"I'm completely incapable of not being nice to you."

Which is why I'm definitely sleeping on this couch tonight.

Even if we didn't have a very large age gap, she's not someone I want to fuck things up with.

Ever.

So I'll take it slow. Keep being nice to her. Keep being the guy she can trust. The guy who doesn't yell at her. And the guy who wants to crawl onto that mattress and kiss the wariness right off her face, but who knows she needs to be the one to make the next move.

I shoot to my feet. "I'm gonna move the chicken to the freezer with the ice. If the power's not back on tomorrow, we can try roasting it over the fire."

She watches me go.

Doesn't say another word.

Doesn't ask me to tell her more about liking her.

Doesn't ask me not to either.

Fucking mouth.

It's gonna be an even longer night tonight.

10

Aspen

IT'S AWKWARD AGAIN, and I'm not sleeping.

Every time I think I might doze off, I start to feel cold, and within seconds—*seconds*—Cash is up putting more wood on the fire, then returning to the couch, where the fake leather gives one singular groan and goes silent, like he's fallen immediately back to sleep.

The way I want to text him right now is overwhelming.

This guy I have an unfortunate crush on told me he likes me too, and now I feel awkward because I want to do something about it, but he's my landlord, and I don't want to lose one more place to live because it got weird between us.

He'd text me back something like *Is it already weird enough to move? If so, seize the day.*

And I'd reply *Might not even matter depending on how long this storm lasts.*

He'd say *YOLO*.

I'd say *I just want him to crawl into bed and snuggle me because it's dark and cold and no matter how much I tell myself that I'm fine by myself, I don't like being alone in the cold and dark.*

There's something about the night that makes everything seem worse.

Like the night is when the bear comes. Or a snow monster. Or the family I walked away from.

And then they're here.

My family.

Marching to the door of my cabin castle, led by the bear who was sent to sniff me out.

You have pebbles! We want pebbles!

I don't have pebbles, I cry.

You made pebbles and you kept them from us! They have guitars that shoot arrows, and they're sending flaming arrows through the air as they advance. *We will burn it all down for you turning your back on us!*

Do your worst! I yell back. *You've made me rise from the ashes before, and I'll do it again!*

"Aspen," a whiskey-smooth voice says beside me. The world shakes, and I hear it again. "*Aspen.*"

I sit straight up with a gasp, the dream clearing, the darkness cut by the glow of the fire coming back into focus.

Cash.

Cash is beside me.

On top of the quilts.

Stroking my back. "Hey. You okay?"

I swipe my nose.

Shit.

I'm crying.

Fucking dream.

"Yeah," I whisper.

He doesn't answer.

Why should he? We both know I'm lying.

"You have bad dreams often?"

I shake my head.

He grunts.

Once again, we both don't believe me.

Have I had bad dreams while we've both been in Malibu at the same time? Does he sleep with his windows open? Could he have heard me if I did?

"You warm enough?" he asks.

I nod, but at the same time, I shiver.

I try not to, but I do. My fingers are cold. My nose is cold. I'm still wiping tears off my face like they're not there.

I hate crying in front of people.

It's weakness.

Also, the streaks where the tears fall are cold.

Fire's a little low again.

He shoves up from the mattress, grabs a log, and tosses it on. We're both silent as it catches, sending a brighter glow through the room. I shift and settle back under the covers. I'm shivering far more than I should be this close to the fire.

And then he does the best-worst thing he can do, and he takes the two quilts he's been using on the couch and shakes them out over the two quilts I'm already using on the mattress.

And then he climbs under the covers with me.

Heat touches my skin as he curls up behind me, one arm looped around my belly.

"Go back to sleep," he says softly. "You're safe. I've got you."

You're safe. I've got you. "People in my life don't say that kind of thing to me," I whisper.

"Then you need better people."

I have better people. Waverly would leap mountains to get here if she knew I needed a friend, and Cooper would be right beside her.

But I don't ask because she's already done so much for me, and I don't want to burden her with the hang-ups that are better saved for a therapist.

I huddle closer to Cash, soaking in his warmth, and settle my hand on his arm, giving it a light *thank you* squeeze.

He yelps softly.

"Sorry. Sorry," I whisper as I release his arm. "My hands are—"

"Freezing," he whispers back.

He grabs my hand and cradles it in his. Warmth seeps into my fingers, and I almost want to cry again.

I like being held. I like being close to people.

But I don't trust it.

That's why I date, but only for short periods of time.

But it's so easy to trust Cash right now.

His breath is warm in my ear as he murmurs, "Is your other hand cold too?"

"No."

"Liar."

"I can't even feel it anymore."

"How are you the closest one to the fire and the colder of the two of us?"

"Talent."

He chuckles, the warm reverberations rumbling against my back. "Give me your other hand."

"Bossy."

"I don't let people freeze on my watch."

"You're keeping the fire going. My poor circulation isn't your fault."

It's not poor circulation.

It's legit that the rest of the house is getting cold and there's only so much that a fire can do.

Cash maneuvers my hands so they both press together against my breasts.

He doesn't touch my breasts himself.

I don't think.

I think that's just my own hands.

And they're warming up.

I curl into a tighter ball and press back against him. Swear I'm seeking warmth and warmth only.

Except his sharp inhale and the very solid ridge against my tailbone tell me I'm getting the full cuddling-with-my-secret-crush-who-likes-me-back experience.

"Sorry," he mutters.

"Fuck sorry," I mutter back, and I press even harder against his erection.

"Aspen—"

"We could freeze to death out here. Do you want your last act on earth to be heroic, or do you want your last act on earth to be the best blaze of glory?"

There's a beat of silence, and then he cracks up. "Quit quoting my most famous movie lines at me."

"Oh, were you in that movie? I forgot."

"Yes, I was in that movie. Lead character. The one who saved the world? Ring a bell?" Fingers brush my breasts, and those are *not* my fingers.

I can tell by the way goosebumps break out all over my chest.

I'm still in my hoodie and sweatpants. He's not touching my skin anywhere except my hands, and I'm still getting delicious chills. "Oh, I might remember that now."

His nose nestles into my hair.

The fire crackles and sends a dancing yellow glow around the room.

My fingers are warming.

My breasts are tingling. My vagina is asking if we're really going to sleep like this, or if we can have other fun first.

"Cash?" I whisper.

"Hmm?"

"My nose is cold too."

He shifts, releasing my hands, and clamps his palm over my nose. "Yep. Definitely cold."

I snort in amusement, my own breath filling his hand and warming my nose up.

But only a little.

I roll over until I'm facing him, and scoot close enough that my hands are scrunched between us, my nose buried in the warm, smoke-and-pancake scent of his T-shirt.

"Aspen—"

"Shh. Conserve energy."

He's stiff against me—his whole body, I mean, not specifically just his penis—but only for a moment.

And then he relaxes.

Except for his penis.

This is such a bad idea.

But it's a much better idea than having more nightmares.

Being cold by myself.

Being alone.

He tugs me tighter against him and presses a kiss to my hair.

I slide my top hand under his shirt and wrap my arm around his back, lying to myself that it's for heat.

His breath hitches again, but he doesn't pull away.

If anything, he tightens his grip on me.

And I feel safe.

So safe.

Cared for.

Cherished.

Especially when he kisses my head again.

"Thank you for being here with me," I whisper.

"Glad to have fucked up in the right way," he murmurs back.

I kiss his chest and burrow closer to him, my fingers cautiously exploring the hot, smooth skin on his back.

He buries his face in my hair, gripping me even tighter.

"Whatever happens here can stay here," I tell his shirt.

"I don't want you to regret anything."

"My entire life is one regret after another. Even if I regret this, it'll be small. Barely noticeable. A little blip."

He goes completely still and silent for a moment.

For the love of guitar strings. "I'm not calling *this* a blip," I add, flexing my hips against his erection.

He coughs. Half laughs. Coughs again. "I didn't think—"

"Yes, you did."

"Maybe a little."

I giggle.

He kisses my forehead.

The way I want to push him onto his back, crawl on top of him, strip out of my clothes, and make love to him is overwhelming.

It's scary—this will change everything, no matter how much I might try to insist that what happens here, stays here—but he's here.

He likes me.

I like him.

I *trust* him.

Screw it.

I might never have this chance again.

11

Cash

THE ONLY REASON I'm not ready to die right now is that when I go, I don't want to go before the woman I've sworn to myself that I'll protect through this.

But there's no small part of me ready to die of utter bliss at the feel of her hands on my bare skin. Her breath warm through my shirt. The press of her lips against my chest.

The real Aspen is better than any fantasy I've had about her the past year.

Her touch. Her scent. The way she's arching into me as she lifts her head to press a kiss to my bare neck.

My dick aches, trapped in my pants. My hands tremble with the desperate need to touch her bare skin. I want to taste her—her body, her mouth, her pussy—everywhere.

"Your nose is warm," I rasp.

"You fixed it." She presses another kiss just below my jawline and hooks one leg around my hips.

They buck in response.

It's primal instinct. "Fuck, Aspen, I don't want to mess this up."

"Being with me? Or our friendship?"

"Yes."

"You are the only man I've ever known who would say something like that to me."

My heart swells and protective instincts take over. Who's been in her life who didn't value her enough to not want to fuck up what they had?

"You need better friends."

"I think I've finally found them." Her lips find my ear, and my cock grows another inch.

It's about to get strangled inside my pants.

"I want you, Cash," she whispers. "Please don't make me beg."

The last shreds of my honor evaporate.

It doesn't matter that I shouldn't want her back. It doesn't matter that there are ten thousand reasons this is a terrible idea.

She wants me, and I won't make her beg.

I claim her mouth with a rough growl, rolling her onto her back and closer to the dancing fire. Her fingers clench my hair as she kisses me back, hard and deep, our tongues clashing, breath mingling, her legs wrapping around my hips.

This.

Heaven help me, *this.*

She's sweet and tart and rich all at once, her body so

soft under mine, her lips and tongue and mouth eager and bold.

I'm never coming back from this.

Just kissing her is making everything in my world shift.

I don't feel like a movie star. I'm not an aging former boy bander.

I'm a man who will do anything to make this woman happy. To give her pleasure. To take away her pain, her fears, her insecurities.

She glides her hands down my chest and pops the button on my pants.

I groan in relief as she slides the zipper down, then fists me in both hands and strokes me.

"My god, you feel good." She strokes harder, her hands trapped between our bodies. "You're bigger than I imagined you'd be."

My eyes cross. I can't catch my breath.

And I will myself not to come in her hands, no matter how good her smooth, warm fingers feel against the steel rod standing in for my cock.

I hold myself above her, careful not to crush her, as I breathe through the desperate need for release.

"Do you ever think about me naked?" she whispers.

"All the damn time."

"Do you touch yourself when you think about me naked?"

"Yes."

"Do you want to see me naked?"

"Aspen."

"Help me take my clothes off, Cash. I want you to strip me bare."

I don't know how any sane man could decline that request. Especially when it's accompanied by a shower of kisses on my neck.

I pull her hand off my cock and shift to hover over her as I guide her arms out of their sleeves, pressing my mouth down her arm as her bare skin is revealed. Then the other arm, tasting every inch of the flesh covering her long, lean forearm and biceps.

Her shoulder.

Her neck.

She squirms and gasps under me as I uncover her breasts—*god*, she's fucking perfect—and then tug her shirts over her head.

I pause to lick her nipple, lit by the glowing embers of the fire, and then the other nipple.

"More," she whimpers.

As if I could deny her anything.

I tease and lick and suck on her breasts, my cock getting impossibly harder at how fucking fantastic it feels to be feasting on Aspen's body.

The way I've fantasized about this a million times over since the first time I realized who was in my pool house…

Aspen in reality is a universe better than Aspen in my fantasies though.

Because this Aspen is gasping and saying my name and gripping my hair and clenching her legs around my hips of her own free will.

In reality.

Not in some made-up fantasy land. It's not a role. It's not a part.

It's her lifting her hips as I hook my thumbs under her sweatpants and panties and tug them down, while I'm still worshipping her plump, firm breasts with the delicious hard, rosy tips.

"Shit," I whisper.

She makes a soft, desperate noise. "What?"

"No condom."

"I'm on birth control. And I haven't—there hasn't been anyone in over a year."

I lift my head to look her square in the eyes. "There hasn't been anyone for me since the first time you texted me."

"Cash," she whispers.

What the hell have I been waiting for? "Tell me to stop, and I'll stop, but my god, Aspen, I've wanted you for so long, this almost doesn't feel real."

"I'll murder you with a wine bottle and leave you out for the bears to eat if you stop."

If my dick wasn't as hard as a frozen lamppost and I wasn't so eager to get back to licking her entire body, that would be funny.

I bury my head between her breasts and kiss her breastbone, then tug her pants down more, until she's squirming beneath me and helping me by kicking them the rest of the way off.

And then she reaches for my shirt.

It goes flying, and I barely have the presence of mind to make sure it's flying *away* from the fire.

Next she tackles my pants, pushing them farther down my hips until my cock springs all the way free.

"Good boy," she says, and once again, I'm smiling as I lick the side of her breast, which makes her suck in a breath while she grips my head again, holding me there to play with her breasts more.

She's fun, and she's also so real. Strong and vulnerable at the same time.

I would slay dragons so she'd never have to hurt again.

"I'm so wet," she gasps as I suckle on her nipple. "I want—I need—Cash, *please.*"

I stroke between her legs, and fuck me, she's soaked. Slick heat coats my fingers.

"*Yes.*" She moans. "Yes, *more.*"

I shift so I'm angled right to kiss her while I circle her clit with my thumb and her legs spread wider.

If you'd told me a week ago that I'd be teasing Aspen's pussy while she arches into my hand, letting me slip my fingers through her folds while my cock aches with the desperate need to be inside of her, skin on skin, mouth to mouth, tongue to tongue, I would've told you to go fuck yourself.

Yet this is real.

She's here, whimpering in my mouth, her body trembling as I play with her clit and thrust my fingers deeper and deeper into her vagina, hips pumping into my hands, until her inner walls clench hard around my fingers.

So.

Fucking.

Immaculate.

I don't care that my balls will be blue for the next three years.

Doesn't matter when I get to watch her throw her head back, neck straining into her release, eyes unfocused, skin glowing in the firelight, knowing I did this.

I made her come.

I gave her ultimate pleasure.

She's mine now.

Fuck anyone who tries to say otherwise.

Including me.

"Oh, god, Cash." She pants as her body relaxes beneath me. "More?"

I chuckle. "More?" I repeat.

"Definitely more." She sucks in one deep breath, blows it out, and takes another. "So much more."

She hooks an arm around my neck, pulling me in for a kiss, my fingers still inside her as her tongue touches mine again.

I love this woman.

I do.

I started falling for her over text. I tried to deny it when I realized how much younger she is, when I knew our schedules wouldn't line up, when I knew there were people in my life who would do worse than knock me out with a wine bottle and feed me to the bears if they knew the number of times I jerked off to images of Aspen's ass, her mouth, her laugh, her breasts, the fantasy of her playing with herself—

I fell harder every minute I spent with her.

And now, being here together, starting to peel back the layers she uses to guard herself—I love her.

I want her.

I would do anything for her.

Absolutely anything.

So when she pushes me onto my back as she's kissing me, I go.

As she strokes my cheeks and kisses me deeper, I kiss her back with everything I have in me.

And as she hovers that sweet pussy over my cock, I let her take her time, teasing my tip with her slick, hot center, until she slides down my dick with that tight, wet pussy hugging me.

Riding me.

Stroking me.

Her breath comes faster.

My heart can't keep up, but my hips buck into her while she makes soft *yes, more, please, right there, don't stop, oh god* noises.

She braces herself, hands on my chest, while she rides me harder and harder, so good, *so fucking good*, her breasts bouncing, her skin glowing in the firelight, driving me closer and closer to climax.

"Come for me again, angel," I say. "Come for me again."

"Cash, I—*oh god*, I'm so close," she pants.

I'm going to blow my load, and fuck if I'll feel old for not being able to hold out long enough to give her another orgasm. "You have the sexiest fucking pussy."

She moans and grinds down on my pelvis.

I buck into her again. "I want to eat it for breakfast."

"Oh, fuck," she gasps.

"I want you to come all over my face."

"*Cash.*"

"And then fuck you in front of a mirror so you can watch."

She whimpers my name again as her walls squeeze and spasm around my cock, and *fuck yes, finally.*

My entire body strains as I let go with a deep groan of relief. Everything inside me tightens and finally releases, dots dancing in my vision as the power of my climax hits me so hard that I feel it in my gut.

"*Yes,*" Aspen croons, still coming all over me while I ride the wave of my own orgasm.

I don't want this to end.

I don't want to ever pull my dick out of her.

I don't want to move.

I just want to stay here, coming so hard my eyes are permanently crossed while this fucking amazing woman collapses on top of me, panting for breath, while I'm still coming.

But the spasms in my cock fade, and soon I'm sagging deeper into the mattress too, my noodle arms barely able to pull the covers back up over us as she snuggles into my chest.

"So much better," she murmurs.

I kiss her hair. Can't find words.

Don't want to.

I just want to be.

I want this to be real.

I want her to love me back.

I want this to be the beginning. Not the end.

And I'm terrified if I move wrong, say the wrong thing, then it'll be the end.

"Better than I dreamed," she murmurs.

My cock twitches like we didn't just give an Olympic-worthy performance.

She's dreamed of me.

I stroke her hair and pull her closer. She's still splayed across me, and my half-limp dick is still partially inside of her.

And I still don't want to move.

I'll have to eventually. The fire will get low. We'll need to both get cleaned up as best we can.

But not yet.

Not yet.

12

Aspen

THERE ARE NO MORE NIGHTMARES.

I don't sleep through the whole night, but anytime I wake up, Cash is there.

He's cradling me from behind, or I'm sleeping with my head on his shoulder, or we're holding hands.

If I get cold, he's curling around me before I realize what's wrong.

If I make a noise, he pulls me closer.

He gets up to put more wood on the fire occasionally, and eventually, I realize the room is light.

It's a dim light—the curtains and blinds are still drawn—but the light making its way through the fabric tells me that the sun has chased the clouds away.

The fire's going bright, as though Cash must've just put another log or two on, but he's curled up behind me again, one hand cupping my breast, his breath warm on my bare shoulder.

I stretch my legs, and his grip tightens.

"Morning," he says softly.

"Morning," I murmur back.

"Can't remember the last time I didn't have to get up and do something."

Translation: don't you dare move, we're staying right here because it's cozy and warm and perfect.

At least, that's how I choose to translate it.

"I don't do lazy well," I tell him.

"You're not being lazy. You're keeping me warm. Essential job. My family thanks you."

He's made sure I'm nearest the fire the entire night.

It's a little thing, but it's not something I take for granted.

"The bigger I get, the more I worry my family will come after me," I whisper.

"I won't let them."

I don't need other people to take care of me.

But I'm starting to believe in the idea that I'm not alone.

I have people in my life that I call friends. People other than Waverly, I mean.

But I don't let them close. Not close enough to tell them why I don't let them close.

It's something of a self-perpetuating circle, and generally, they move on after a few years. It's the way of things, and I've accepted it.

Until now.

Now, I don't want to move on to a different friend

group. I want to stay here, with Cash. I want to know that eventually, when the power comes back on, I can call Waverly and she'll worry and then I'll tell her a bear got into Cash's car and we'll both laugh about it.

Once we're safe.

Once the power's back on and the driveway is clear.

"You don't even know why that's a bad thing," I say to Cash.

"Don't need specifics. I just need to know you don't want them to come after you. PS, family should never come after you. That's not how family's supposed to work."

"Did you really just say *PS*?"

"All the young people are doing it."

I smile at the fire and stroke my fingers up and down his arm.

I like his arm. It's strong and sinewy, with wiry light brown hairs all over it giving it a rough texture.

He kisses my shoulder, and I doze back to sleep.

I don't know how much time passes before I realize he's up again, adding more logs to the fire. The room's even brighter now.

"Hungry?" he asks me.

My stomach answers for me.

He's pulled his pants and shirt back on. I tell myself it's for warmth, and he'll get naked with me again, but I don't know for sure.

"You want cheese and carrots, or do you want to eat blindfolded and have something that you'd rather not realize you're eating?" he asks me.

Sweet man doesn't want to feed me a gingerbread

house if he thinks it'll make me upset. "I'll have whatever you're having."

"Boozy truffles for breakfast it is."

I reach for my hoodie, but he makes a noise.

I lift a brow at him.

"Can I watch you eat naked?"

My vagina clenches in anticipation and my breasts tingle in excitement. "You want to see this?" I ask, giving him a peek at one nipple.

His Adam's apple bobs and he adjusts himself in his pants as he looks down at me. "Yes. But not if you're cold."

I push up to sitting and let the quilts fall to my waist. "I think I'll be okay."

He stares at my breasts.

I rub my hands under them, then pinch my nipples.

"Fuck, Aspen," he rasps.

"Bring the boozy chocolates."

It's amusing that he thinks he's too old for me when he can move that fast.

One moment, I'm watching his ass in his jeans, and the next, he's kneeling at the foot of the bed, stripped down himself, and crawling up to me with a box of truffles in one hand.

Tight muscles cover his shoulders and chest, and his erection stands tall and proud from a thatch of light brown hair. I reach for it as he holds a truffle to my mouth.

His eyes cross, and he swipes the chocolate over my cheek.

"Fuck. Sorry," he mutters.

I giggle.

And when he offers me the truffle again, I suck his fingers into my mouth with the chocolate treat.

His cock twitches in my hand.

I squeeze it lightly, then stroke it up and down, watching his eyes slide shut as he pulls his fingers out of my mouth. "Aspen..."

"Nowhere to go," I whisper. "All we have to do is stay warm today."

He growls, and then the man has his face between my thighs, doing exactly what he promised last night and eating me for breakfast.

His tongue on my seam, his lips sucking on my clit, his fingers teasing my inner thighs—it's not thirty seconds before I'm coming in a blindingly hot flash of heaven.

And as I'm lying there panting, he looks up at me and smirks.

Smirks.

Like *I told you so* or something.

"You're—really good—at that," I pant. "Did you—practice—on a—watermelon?"

He dips his head to my stomach and laughs.

I could lie here forever, running my fingers through his hair, my body warm from the afterglow of an orgasm.

But it doesn't work that way when the power's out, apparently.

He snags the covers and pulls them up over both of us as he settles next to me, pressing kisses to my shoulder and neck.

"I like you," he murmurs.

"I like you too," I whisper back while I arch into his erection again.

We both fall silent, letting our hands and our bodies do the talking as I hook a leg around his hip and scoot closer, rubbing my pussy against his cock again.

He holds my gaze as he slides into me, silently asking all of the questions.

Is this okay? Are you okay? Do you want more? Oh, right there, hmm? This too?

I can't remember the last time I had four orgasms in under twelve hours, but here we are, with me biting his shoulder as I come hard and fast again, my body responding like this is what it's been missing my entire life.

How is it so easy to be with him?

Is this the snowed-in effect?

Is it the fire?

Or is it simply *him*?

While we lie panting, limbs still tangled, both of us still on our sides, he once again pulls me closer.

I don't date guys who pull me closer. I date guys who get off, say things like *thanks, love, let's do that again soon*, and get back up and go about their days.

But Cash—he's sighing that bone-deep, contented sigh as I snuggle closer against his body.

If the real world didn't exist, if we didn't eventually have to leave here—possibly on foot to get to the nearest cabin through the snow if we run out of firewood—I'd let myself be happy.

Believe in this.

But I know it can't last forever.

Especially when his stomach grumbles too.

"Possibly that was more of a workout than breakfast?" I tease.

He shifts, leaning over me to grab the chocolates, then settles back in close.

He feeds me one first, then pops one in his own mouth. "I haven't had candy for breakfast since I was a kid."

"Living on the edge out here."

"I'll be hyped up like a chipmunk in the next thirty minutes."

I lean my head against his chest and listen to his heartbeat.

It's music.

The best kind of music.

"You need your journal?" he asks after a while.

Huh.

I don't.

Not at all, in fact. Not even to write down how amazing this has been.

I don't want to vomit these moments out of my brain.

I want to keep living in them.

He plays with my hair. I trace patterns on his chest.

This, my heart whispers again. *This is what's missing.*

We lie like this for hours, but eventually, we're both starving enough to get up for real food. While we roast chicken strips over the fire with the longest silverware we can find, we make small talk until small talk turns to real talk.

I tell him a few of the shorter stories about why I hate the holidays.

He tells me he's getting tired of Hollywood, and also

that I should spend time with his family at weird holidays like Groundhog Day and Talk Like a Pirate Day since everyone deserves a holiday they love.

I tell him I'm afraid I'll be a one-hit wonder.

While several of my songs have charted, they haven't charted *high*.

Not like "Forget Christmas."

"You'll hit with another song." His voice is rough whiskey, and I want to drown in it.

"Another Christmas song," I mutter as I test my chicken. Not quite done.

He snorts in amusement. "So don't record more."

"What if that's all that my audience wants from me though? What if I'm Mariah Carey but without the rest of her catalog?"

"Do you want to keep recording normal-time songs?"

"*Yes*." I love performing. I love singing. I don't care if there's one person or a thousand in the audience. "But if I'm a one-hit wonder with a Christmas song, I'm done. I'll go back to remote jobs and find a new hobby and squat in your pool house forever."

"You are not a one-hit wonder." He pauses in roasting his own chicken to tuck a lock of hair behind my ears, and I get a whole-body shiver at his touch.

The good kind of whole-body shiver. "I don't think you understand the way my karma works in the universe. It's so bad, I was probably one of those people in a previous life who lived to yuck other people's yums and always left grocery carts in the middle of the parking lot even though I was able-bodied enough to return them to the cart holders."

His gaze drops to my lips.

My belly drops to the floor.

I shouldn't want him to kiss me again. We've already made this more complicated for when we go back to the real world.

But I feel so safe here with him.

Cherished. Appreciated. Adored.

"Some people get all of their hard parts out of the way early in life," he says. "That's you. You've gotten the hard things out of the way, and everything from here on out is clear skies and smooth sailing."

"Your confidence is adorable."

"There's this thing that when you get snowed in with someone, you swap luck. I have the best family. Great friends. Already had two great careers. Still have time to find another if I want. When we get out of here, you're taking all of my luck with you. Your everyday songs are gonna explode, Aspen. You'll find the people you call family. And you'll be happy."

My heart is a jackhammer trying to get through my breastbone. I want to believe him. I want to believe him so badly it hurts.

But more, I want to kiss him.

I want to kiss him more than I want to breathe.

Again.

"It doesn't work like that."

He smiles at me. "I look forward to the day you eat those words."

I'm looking forward to being trapped here with him for a few more days.

Because here, I *can* kiss him.

Here, I *can* believe he wants to be one of those people I call family. That he wants to be one of those people who call me family.

That our friendship is supposed to progress this way forever.

And that I don't have to be afraid.

13

Cash

THE POWER STAYS off all day, but it's still the good kind of day.

The best, actually.

Kissing.

Sex.

She pulls out her guitar. She sings for me. I take it and sing for her.

Old stuff.

Bro Code stuff with lyrics changed that has her laughing so hard she cries.

We peek out the windows, and she gets teary-eyed again.

Not because the three feet or so of snow on the ground is trapping us here either.

"It's even prettier than in the movies," she whispers.

"You've never seen this much snow?"

She shakes her head, and I get the joy of watching her soak in the wonder of something beautiful and new. "I wish I brought clothes for a snowball fight."

I promise her there's far more fun to be had in the snow than a simple snowball fight, and I'm not just talking about sex in an igloo.

She teases me about being a big kid at heart.

Not wrong.

Now, once again, we're snuggled on the mattress in front of the fire as the clock creeps later and later. I don't want to panic her, but we're starting to run low on firewood. We can make it through tonight, possibly into tomorrow morning, but not much longer.

If the power doesn't come back on, we'll have to try hiking out.

But that's a problem for tomorrow.

Tonight, I'm soaking up every minute of being with this woman.

Touching her. Tasting her. Talking to her.

Dozing off.

Waking up to put more wood on the fire.

Crawling back into bed with Aspen.

If she has any more nightmares, they don't wake her, and she doesn't tell me about them.

She does curl into me and rub my back and squeeze my ass and stroke my cock though.

By the time morning comes, I don't know if I've slept or not, and I don't care.

For the first time in years, I feel rested.

Bone-deep rested.

Happy.

But that's before the sound of a chainsaw rips through the air.

It's muffled—clearly outside—but that is definitely a chainsaw.

Aspen jolts straight upright at the noise. "What?" she gasps.

"Stay. I'll check it out."

I grab my pants and head for the window, where I'm equal parts surprised and not surprised by what I see.

It's Davis, in front of a truck with a snowplow, tackling the tree that fell and blocked the driveway the other night. Even bundled up in a coat and stocking cap, it's easy to tell it's Davis.

One, takes a big stocking cap to cover his man bun, and two, that's definitely his beard.

"Rescue's here," I say to Aspen as someone else knocks on the door.

She makes a noise, then ducks under the covers.

I pull on my shirt and head to the door, where I find —*shit*.

Cooper.

He's in a big winter coat and snow boots too, though his head is bare.

"Little weather trouble out here?" he says with a grin that I don't entirely trust.

I've been playing hide the sausage with a woman his girlfriend cares about, and it won't take him long to figure that out.

"Little bit," I say.

"Power should be back on—now." He grins wider as a

soft *pop* sounds behind me, and then the overhead light blinks on.

Aspen peeks out from under the covers, sucks in an audible breath, and dives back under the quilts.

"*Shower,*" I hear her whisper.

Cooper looks at me.

Then angles his head toward the interior of the cabin.

"Just you two?" I ask him with a nod to Davis. "Let me grab my coat. I can help shovel."

Cooper doesn't move.

Dude takes his time crossing his arms over his chest and looking at me.

"Don't be an ass," Aspen calls from under the covers.

"There's only one woman in the world who can tell me that, and you're not her," he replies.

"Does Waverly know you still only take orders from your mother?" Aspen retorts.

Cooper cracks a grin, looks at me, and goes straight-faced again. "Why are you here?"

"Don't answer that," Aspen orders.

Cooper's nose twitches like he can smell what we've been up to.

"Cabin's on a well," I tell him. "No power, no water. And the chicken almost went bad."

"That doesn't answer why you're here."

"I've been ordered to not tell you."

We have a stare-down.

"You two asshats gonna keep staring lovingly into each other's eyes, or are you gonna get out here and help with the snow?" Davis calls.

"They didn't send a helicopter?" Aspen's voice is still muffled under the covers.

Cooper half snorts, then frowns like he didn't consider the helicopter, then finally grins again. "We don't love him *that* much."

"Davis needs to keep himself busy or he gets in trouble," I add.

"Huh," Aspen says. "That makes sense. Cooper too."

The back door of the extended cab with the snowplow opens, and Waverly pokes her own beanie-covered head out.

"Is Aspen in there? Is she okay?"

Aspen sticks her head all the way out of the quilts but keeps her neck and shoulders covered.

"Was that Waverly?"

Cooper leans past me to look at her. "Yeah, she wanted to check on you herself, but she can't get through the snow yet."

Aspen's eyes get shiny. "Then get to work."

I'm already grabbing my coat and boots.

Davis is alternating between clearing snow off the fallen tree and cutting segments of it to clear the road. I start shoveling a path to the cars. Cooper wades through the nearly waist-high snow to get back to the truck, then returns to join me with a second shovel.

Waverly follows him and heads into the cabin in the path his longer legs made.

I hear a shriek, and then rapid-fire talking, and I can't stop a smile despite the growing dread in my chest.

We're getting our rescue.

Power's back on.

Aspen will be able to get to the store.

She doesn't need me here anymore.

So is this it?

Is this the end?

Or is this the beginning?

"You didn't do anything I'll have to kick your ass for, did you?" Cooper asks me while I shovel.

"Nope." Yep.

"You know I'm going to take Waverly's word for the answer to that more than yours, right?"

"I'd kick your ass if you didn't."

He pauses with the shovel in the snow and props his arms on it. "Why'd you come out here?"

"Wrong answers only?"

"Aspen's like another sister to me, except I like her more than my real sister, and most of the time, I like my real sister a hell of a lot," he reminds me.

Fuck.

I think I owe him the truth.

Especially since he's out here digging me out as much as he's digging Aspen out.

"I thought I scared her away from Beck's party, so I came to apologize."

"How?"

"By saying I'm sorry."

"How'd you scare her away, jackass?"

"Turns out I didn't." No, I've put the pieces together the past couple days, and I realized it was her song.

Not me.

She would've kissed me.

She *has* kissed me.

This attraction isn't one-sided.

"Why'd you think you did?" Cooper asks.

"More shoveling, less gabbing," Davis calls.

Cooper picks up a scoopful, still eyeing me.

"She's fucking amazing," I mutter.

"Duh. Waverly doesn't make friends with people who aren't."

I eye the baseball player.

He grins, clearly not at all ashamed of his own ego lingering in that statement. *I'm awesome too because Waverly hangs out with me.*

But then he goes serious. "You like her."

"I liked her before I ever met her. We started texting when she moved into my pool house."

Cooper snorts.

Helpful. "What?"

"You're welcome."

I stop shoveling and stare at him. *"You're welcome?"*

"Dude. Do you know how many times Waverly's like, 'Oh, Aspen's texting with Cash again'? Like *every day.* You think the rest of us don't know?"

Not just staring anymore. Now, I'm gaping.

He levels me with another *be fucking for real* look. "Why do you think we invited her to Beck's party?"

"Quit telling him all of our secrets, dumbass," Davis says.

"You knew," I say to Cooper.

"You're not exactly subtle, my dude."

I look back at the cabin.

Is Waverly having the same conversation with Aspen?

"More shoveling," Davis says.

We both put our heads down over our shovels and get back to work.

My friends knew.

All of them knew I had a crush on Aspen.

No wonder Waverly didn't blink when I said I needed to get Aspen some stuff she left behind at Beck's house.

Did she know Aspen liked me too?

Having Davis and Cooper here makes the past two days feel like a dream. Not like reality.

But could it be reality?

Were they actually playing wingmen, and I didn't know it?

Fuck.

This is why I've kept shit casual since my short-lived wedding to a fan fifteen years ago. Because I read things wrong.

But I know what I want.

I *want* Aspen.

I think there's a chance she wants me too.

So we'll see where we go from here.

I hope it's somewhere good. I'd hate to lose one of my favorite friends.

14

Aspen

BEFORE WAVERLY GETS INSIDE, I give myself a quick cold washcloth bath and change clothes, then shove the quilts that smell like sex into the bedroom.

And then I get to enjoy my friend. She's everything I need at this moment.

She shrieks with laughter and gasps in horror at all of the right spots as I tell her about the past few days. And when I whisper that I think I have a crush on Cash, she's not horrified.

She just grins bigger and says, "Finally figured that out, did you?"

Apparently I talk about him a lot.

"I don't date seriously," I tell Waverly as we move the mattress back into the bedroom since the power's on again. "It's not my thing."

"It can be," is all she says before the men come filing back into the house.

We've kept the fire going, and they huddle around it.

"Road's clear," Cooper tells Waverly. "Come warm my hands up to reward me for doing such a good job."

"He didn't clear the road," Cash says.

Waverly's laughing as she leans into Cooper and takes his hands in hers, blowing on them. "I'm well aware."

"I was great emotional support, and I shoveled like a champ," he says proudly.

Cash meets my eyes and rolls his.

I want to crack up, but I'm suddenly so nervous about having other people here that the laughter dies in my throat.

"Brought fresh firewood," Davis says. He's always so quiet that it's weird when you hear him speak. "Cleaned out Beck's secret holiday stash too."

Cash and I both jerk our heads at him. "You too?" I say as Cash says, "He already refilled it?"

Davis smirks. "Levi's cleaning him out tomorrow. This is fun."

Cash snickers.

Glances at me, pulls a face that clearly says *shit, now you have to deal with more holiday stuff*, then looks at Davis again.

Davis smirks. "Didn't, actually. He cried too much when he saw what you stole, and I'm too nice to do that to him right after he got it refilled."

I don't think Beck actually cried.

Probably not.

It's highly unlikely. I think.

But more definitive—our rescuers did, in fact, bring food. We have a charcuterie lunch feast with a side of sprinkle pancakes that Cash insists on making for me.

Waverly and I share a bottle of wine.

The house starts warming up again.

And as the last of the meats and cheeses and olives and pickles and grapes disappear, it quickly becomes obvious that it's time for the people who are leaving to leave.

Davis gives a subtle head jerk to Cooper that all of us recognize as *time to hit the road*.

"Are you staying?" Waverly asks me.

I slide a glance at Cash, then quickly back to her when I realize he's not looking at me. "I think so," I say. "I need to run to the store"—and probably hit a laundromat for the quilts—"but it's nice here."

At least, it has been.

I steal another look at Cash, but Cooper's asking him something, and once again, he's not looking at me.

Waverly looks over at them too. She slips her hand into mine and squeezes. "And are you staying alone?" she murmurs.

"He likes the holidays," I whisper. "He should be with the people who want to celebrate with him. We can...talk later."

There have been three times that Waverly has given me the same *what the fuck is wrong with you?* look that I'm getting now.

First, when I told her she should have a hot public fling with Davis Remington, which is hilarious in retrospect. Second, when I told her I didn't want to stay at her house but wanted to live in a hotel instead right before she hooked me up with staying at Cash's pool house. And the third time was when I told her I hated my Christmas song.

She came around on the last one when she understood why.

But she knows I like Cash. She knows he's indicated he likes me too.

"Do you want to be completely alone, or do you just want to not be around holiday lights and your song?" she whispers.

I look at Cash once more.

This time, he's looking back at me.

Wary brown eyes.

Hopeful?

Is there hope in there?

Does he want to stay?

Does he want me to go home with him?

My stomach ties itself in sloshy knots.

The wine and cheese and meats and olives were not my best idea.

Waverly squeezes my arm. "Call me when you're back in town. We'll pretend it's Fourth of July and go somewhere tropical so we think it's summer."

She and Cooper join Davis in heading for the door.

"Your car's trashed," Davis says to Cash.

"It's Waylon's."

"Your car is trashed, and you're fucked when you explain it to your brother," Davis amends. "You want a ride?"

Cash looks at me.

My heart starts a slow climb up to jackhammer territory.

I swallow.

I don't want things to be awkward between us. I want things to be exactly the way they were eight hours ago, when we were snuggling under the quilts in front of the fire, whispering and touching and kissing.

"Do you want me to—" he starts as I blurt, "Stay."

He sucks in a quick breath.

"If you want," I add.

"Do you want?"

"I don't know how to make a good snowball, and I don't know when I'll get another chance to learn."

He studies me, those warm brown eyes searching mine. "You haven't lived if you haven't built a snow fort in this kind of snow."

"I don't know how to do that either."

"Have you ever been sledding?"

I shake my head.

"Made snow angels?"

I shake my head again. "I need to learn how to winter. But if you want to spend the holidays with your family—"

"Family's what you make it. Do you want me to stay?"

Nodding is one of the scariest, but also rightest, things I've ever done. I *don't* do relationships. I *don't* put myself out on a limb, begging for love.

But I don't think Cash would ever make me beg.

Not for anything.

Everything he's done, from our first text message through these past few days, has been freely offered with no expectations.

My eyes get hot as I nod again. "I want you to stay."

I don't know which one of us takes the first step, but it doesn't matter.

What matters is that I'm throwing myself at him and he's catching me and holding me and pressing his lips to my face.

"You're sure?" he asks.

"*Yes.*"

"I wouldn't want him without clean clothes," Davis mutters.

"Definitely needs a shower," Cooper agrees.

"And neither one of them are going to the store without getting mobbed."

"I think they can figure this out," Waverly says while Cash hugs me and I pepper his face with kisses right back.

I want this.

I want *him*.

I don't care if he's a few years older. I don't care if we need to work out our schedules. I don't care what anyone else thinks.

I just know that for the first time in my life, I believe someone loves me enough to put me first.

Loves me.

He doesn't have to say it.

Not when I can feel it.

"You can go see your family if you want," I tell him again. "I'll be here."

"I want *you* to be part of my family," he replies. "Fuck the traditions. I just want you."

"That's our cue," Waverly whispers. "Go on. Move. Let them have their time."

I don't hear the door shut.

I'm too distracted by kissing Cash.

My holiday miracle.

The man who saved my Christmas merely by wanting me.

Just like I wrote in my song.

"This doesn't feel real," he murmurs to me as he sets me back on the floor, pressing a line of kisses down my neck.

"It feels amazing," I whisper back. "Don't ever stop, okay? I think I'd break if you stop."

"I love you too much to break you."

I believe him.

I have every reason not to, but I do.

I believe him.

And I never want to be alone on the holidays again. Not if I can have Cash with me instead.

EPILOGUE

ONE YEAR LATER...

Cash Rivers, aka a man who's given up Hollywood to go back on the road

IT'S ALMOST midnight on the last day of the best year of my life.

My girlfriend is laughing with her bestie by the bonfire where all of my friends and family members and their kids and parents are gathered roasting marshmallows.

And I'm happy.

There's no other word for it beyond blissfully happy.

When I told Aspen last year as we cuddled at her cabin hideaway that I didn't have any movie sets I had to get to and that I wanted to go on the road with her, I thought for a hot second she'd throw me out.

Tell me it was too much.

Too fast.

Too soon.

Instead, we've been more or less inseparable for a full year now. She rearranged a few shows so she could hit the red carpet with me for the two movie premieres I had the first half of the year, and otherwise, I've followed her wherever she's gone.

"You have any more problems with her family?" Davis asks me.

He's having a holiday kombucha while the two of us watch everyone else having fun. Last year we got a blizzard. This year it's unseasonably warm and we're partying outside.

Weather, man.

"I think they got the message," I reply.

"Good."

Getting to know all of Aspen's secrets has been an exercise in restraint. The more she tells me about how she grew up and some of the situations she found herself in once she left home, the more I want to go complete caveman on anyone who so much as looks at her wrong.

Most days, though, giving her my family and friends to have as her own and supporting her in expanding the small circle she'd started in the music industry before she moved into my pool house has felt like the more important part of my job when it comes to her happiness and well-being.

Watching her relax and be herself more and more with all of them has also been one of my biggest sources of joy.

She deserves so much better than what she grew up with, and now she's getting it.

She laughs again, this time so hard she hiccups.

I'm on instant alert, worried she'll hurt herself, but she's fine. It's just Aspen being about as happy as I've ever seen her.

And she was pretty fucking happy the past week while we recreated our snowed-in experience over last year's holidays.

The only time I've seen her not happy was when I told her we'd skip Beck's New Year's party.

You're giving up the rest of your holiday for my ridiculous insistence on holding on to old memories. We're not skipping Beck and Sarah's New Year's party.

She knows they moved the date to New Year's from the week before Christmas to accommodate her, which she told me was unnecessary.

But she also hugged Sarah tight and told her thank you.

And she played her viral holiday hit from last year for me every day that we were out in the cabin, where we *didn't* lose power this year, and where we did have enough food, and where we celebrated the fact that my lady is no one-hit wonder.

Every last one of her singles landed near the top of the charts, with her last two hitting number one. Her career is exploding, just like we all predicted.

She insists we're spending next year with my family at Christmas, *no matter what*. Because *I love you enough to get over myself for you*. She also tells me every day that even if it all goes away, she's enjoying this ride for exactly what it is.

"Cash! Cash, come see what Zoe taught Commander Crumpet," Aspen calls.

She doesn't have to ask me twice.

Not for anything.

I head over and join their little circle where Zoe orders the hedgehog to go to sleep as she's holding him.

Instead of sleeping, the little creature throws his hands out in the air and sticks his tongue out.

Everyone watching cracks up and praises the little guy for obeying orders.

Aspen slips her arm around my waist and goes up on tiptoe to press a kiss to my cheek. "Have I told you how much I love your family?"

"Yes, but you shouldn't say it around them. They might get big heads."

"You're so cringe, Uncle Cash," Zoe says.

"Do you know what that means?" I whisper to Aspen. I overheard the younger kids talking about *Utah fit check* earlier and wasn't honestly sure if it was good or bad, given the context.

"It means she loves you," Aspen whispers back.

Zoe makes a noise that tells me she definitely doesn't mean she loves me.

Her younger brother comes charging through, and I snag him by the back of the collar before he gets too close to the fire. "Other way, Hudson."

"*Skibidi toilet GYAT!*" he yells, then heads back the other way.

"I don't remember this from last year," I murmur to Aspen.

"It's because you're old and your memory's going," Levi tells me.

"He remembered your birthday this year," Aspen points out.

"He forgot the words to 'America's Sweetheart' yesterday."

Aspen laughs.

She knows I didn't forget the words.

I've spent so much time entertaining myself with alternate lyrics that I slipped into them instead of the original words for our Bro Code debut hit.

"Good point," she says. "I should take him home and get him to bed. Old man bedtime and all that."

I'd object, but I never object to going to bed with Aspen.

"What time is it? Where am I? Am I wearing pants?" I intone.

Someone asked me right after we went public if being with her made me feel younger.

It doesn't.

Being with her makes me feel lighter. But not younger. I don't think about how old either of us are much anymore. We're too busy having fun to worry about that.

"Seriously, though, dude," Levi says, "when are you releasing that album?"

I slide a look at Aspen.

She shakes her head. *Wasn't me.*

"When I get phone calls asking why Cash Rivers is in a studio and I'm still not..." Levi adds.

"Fucking big mouth."

Aspen introduced me to her producer, who didn't tell

me my songs suck, and it's been fun being in the booth again myself.

Still not ready to own them in public though.

"You should glitter bomb him," Aspen murmurs.

I choke on a laugh.

"Don't say that any louder around here," Levi mutters.

She giggles.

Her best friend might have made a point with her prank-pulling boyfriend this past year that involved the glitter bomb to end all glitter bombs.

Beck's house was collateral damage, and while Beck and Cooper's houses are technically neighboring houses, it's not like they can look out their windows and see each other out here.

Hella impressive glitter bomb.

"But also," Aspen says, "you should release your album."

I pull a face.

She squeezes my waist tighter. "When you're ready."

I'll be ready soon.

It's hard to stay scared of rejection when I'm surrounded by this much love every day. No matter what happens with my album in public, Aspen likes it.

And I had a hell of a good time recording it.

That matters most.

"Hey, hey, look what time it is," Beck calls.

The space gets instantly brighter with a couple dozen phones getting pulled out to check the time.

Almost midnight.

"Gotta go find my wife," Levi says.

"You want champagne?" I ask Aspen.

She shakes her head. "Nope. Just you."

Soon, we're counting down the seconds.

And then, at the stroke of midnight, I'm kissing the love of my life.

It's been the best year.

And next year will be even better.

PIPPA GRANT BOOK LIST

The Girl Band Series (Complete)
Mister McHottie

Stud in the Stacks

Rockaway Bride

The Hero and the Hacktivist

The Thrusters Hockey Series
The Pilot and the Puck-Up

Royally Pucked

Beauty and the Beefcake

Charming as Puck

I Pucking Love You

The Bro Code Series
Flirting with the Frenemy

America's Geekheart

Liar, Liar, Hearts on Fire

The Hot Mess and the Heartthrob

Snowed in with Mr. Heartbreaker

The Pretend Fiancé Fiasco

Copper Valley Fireballs Series (Complete)
Jock Blocked

Real Fake Love

ABOUT THE AUTHOR

Pippa Grant wanted to write books, so she did.

Before she became a *USA Today* and #1 Amazon best-selling romantic comedy author, she was a young military spouse who got into writing as self-therapy. That happened around the time she discovered reading romance novels, and the two eventually merged into a career. Today, she has more than 30 knee-slapping Pippa Grant titles and nine published under the name Jamie Farrell.

When she's not writing romantic comedies, she's fumbling through being a mom, wife, and mountain woman, and sometimes tries to find hobbies. Her crowning achievement? Having impeccable timing for telling stories that will make people snort beverages out of their noses. Consider yourself warned.

Find Pippa at...
www.pippagrant.com
pippa@pippagrant.com

Made in United States
Troutdale, OR
11/25/2024

25185327R00099